Lindz McLeod

Copyright © 2024 Lindz McLeod
Cover Art © 2024 Evangeline Gallagher
First published in 2024 by Hedone Books
ISBN (ebook) 978-1-998851-73-7
ISBN (paperback) 978-1-998851-79-9

All rights reserved.

The characters and events portrayed in this book are fictitious. Any similarity to real persons, living or dead, is coincidental and not intended by the authors.

No part of this book may be reproduced, or stored in a retrieval system, or transmitted in any form or by any means, electronic, mechanical, photocopying, recording, or otherwise, without express written permission of the publisher.

To all the worms.

CONTENTS

Content Warning	vii
Chapter 1	1
Chapter 2	7
Chapter 3	15
Chapter 4	23
Chapter 5	29
Chapter 6	35
Chapter 7	43
Chapter 8	51
Chapter 9	57
Chapter 10	63
Chapter 11	73
Chapter 12	81
Chapter 13	87
Chapter 14	93
Acknowledgments	99
About the Author	101
Detailed Content Warnings	103

CONTENT WARNING

CONTENT WARNING

The story that follows may contain graphic violence and gore.

Please go to the very back of the book for more detailed content warnings.

Beware of spoilers.

CHAPTER ONE

As usual, we're forced to retreat into the burrow just before dawn. I linger at the edge of the rough-hewn hole, desperate to see a single glimpse of the first pink finger of the sun slithering over the horizon, but Eilidh tugs me in after her. "Careful, Soph," she hisses. "You know we can't take risks now that Beltane has passed."

She has a point, but I still resent the cold fingers wrapped around my wrist. Our bare feet thump on twelve compacted earthen stairs before the floor slopes steeply into darkness and safety. The burrow has become more like a warren over the past three years; we dug tunnels to connect chambers and ventricles, forming a great, unbeating heart. Often, we lost people to collapses, to unsafe structures with unseen fractures. Not as often as we lost people to the Sunbathers above, but even so, the death toll is both high and unavoidable–cave-ins, disease, madness—all rife down here, where the blackness is absolute. We dare not risk a single light, not even in our deepest caverns.

Christ, how I miss the sunrise.

I follow Eilidh down the lefthand tunnel which leads to our den, where we'd left Old Jeff, Cygnet, and Maya last night. It had been our turn to venture out, to gather what fruit we could from the trees, what stores we could scavenge from what the Sunbathers had left amongst their still-smoldering campsites. It had been a good haul, too; I'd found a still-spitted roast chicken while Eilidh had picked an armful of ripe peaches from the trees overhead. Ahead of me, Eilidh hums softly. True silence is rare here—we're encouraged to communicate our presence to avoid collisions, and every scuff and scuttle is clearly audible. Without sight to guide us, we've made use of our other senses as best we can.

Eilidh hums again, upticking at the end. Fighting back a sigh, I hum to let her know I'm still here—though, where else would I be? She reaches back and gropes for my hand. I allow her a single, brief squeeze before I pull away. She's become more clingy of late, a development I loathe, but the more I displayed my disdain, the clingier she became. I've settled for tolerating small amounts in the hopes that this will slow down the inevitable parasitism.

A few seconds later, we reach the den, where three voices murmur welcomes. I kneel, lowering my goods to the floor. An unwelcome hand touches my shoulder, the fingers scuttling cancrine down to my wrist. I smack it away.

"What smell good?" Cygnet's voice is hungry and laced with hope.

"It's animal, right?" Maya is so fucking paranoid these days. "Like, definitely animal?"

"Last I checked," the smile in Eilidh's voice is practically visible, "people don't have wings."

"Chicken?" Old Jeff's voice is more gravelly than usual, a distinct slug of phlegm coating each word. "Been a long time since I 'ad chicken."

The harvest is carefully laid out and parceled out, piece by piece. Everyone fingers everyone else's food—the darkness doesn't make that any less disgusting. I already ate above ground, like I usually do to avoid such an unhygienic mess: a single chicken leg, accompanied by three sticky-sweet peaches, washed down with tepid water still warm from the sun. We hide full bottles in various places at night, so that the sun can purify them during the day. This reduces the number of bacteria, since without the ability to boil water underground, we're stuck using rudimentary methods. We can't light a fire in the deepest parts of the burrow for myriad reasons: the smoke inhalation, to say nothing of the signal it would send to any nearby Sunbathers. They've been known to root people out from the shallows or cave in the deeper tunnels from above, then pull bodies from the rubble afterwards. We can't light a fire near the entrance for the same reasons, plus there is always the possibility, no matter how unlikely, that a Sunbather might find a way to protect themselves. If they could ever figure out a way to reach us down here, we'd be sitting ducks. Only the darkness saves us, and only the darkness makes us what we are.

Human. Weak. Prey.

"Amazing," Cygnet mumbles through a mouthful.

I can't stand the sounds of other people eating, the sickly washing machine squelching of roiling, syncopated mastication. Even in the old days, I preferred to eat alone, and darkness only enhances the terrible noises. I retreat into the tunnel while they chomp away on our bounty, and instead listen to the faint hums coming from further up, where the tunnels diverge. The right-hand fork leads to another community, a larger one. A splinter group which cleaved from an even bigger crowd a year ago, though none of them will say why. One of them used to screw me occasionally, above and below. Rose or Roz or something. Her freckles, seen by moonlight, looked like a hundred decimal points, separating wholes from fractions. Everything is so delineated these days: day and night, us and them, living and dying. I took every opportunity I could to blur the lines. She's dead now, whatever her name is. After a cave-in, I found a freckled foot spitted over a campfire. I'm never sure whether Eilidh didn't guess about my little tryst or just chose to turn a deaf ear. My girlfriend either thinks about things too much or too little; I've never been able to figure out which it is.

Eilidh has no freckles. Not a single mole adorns her pale curves. When she kisses me I taste pure navy. She's no indigo, tainted with the barest hint of a passionate crimson, nor the dulled sea-glass palate of an Aegean blue. She's an empty night sky or an ocean trench under my dangling feet. A bowl curving over the world, or a slow licking tide, devouring it inch by inch. Never something as complicated as a horizon, as a boundary between one place and the next. She's too much for me and also somehow not enough.

Sometimes I think I hate her. Sometimes I think I hate myself.

"Darling," she calls after a few minutes. "We're finished." I slide back into the den, into the smoggy clouds of other people's breath and belches and worse.

"I 'ave to pee," Old Jeff whines.

"You should have gone before. It's already dawn." Maya heaves a long-suffering sigh.

"Here, use bottle," Cygnet offers, their accent clipped. They won't tell anyone where they're from—as if we have the luxury of being xenophobic these days—but when they dream-talk it's all *kurwa* and *pomoc* and *matka* so it's not as if they're actually fooling anybody. "No spill, okay? Okay?"

I scowl in the darkness. Great, another night breathing his piss fumes when he inevitably misses or splashes it everywhere. It's bad enough that we have to give Old Jeff a portion of our meals when he doesn't contribute anything but stink, hasn't even been outside in weeks. Underneath the smell of hot, sour breath and stale body odor, the cloying stench of decay permeates everything. He's dying, and we all know it. One careless step, one infected cut, one swollen foot. There's only so much that herbs and clean water can handle, and Old Jeff is way beyond help. Though I admit that even if we had proper medicine, I wouldn't waste it on him. *Goddamned old leech. What happened to elders walking out into the storm so that they're no longer burdens on the young and healthy?*

Eilidh winds her arms around me, forcing me into a spooning position. "Hey, babe. Are you okay?"

The wool of her sweater rasps against my own scavenged garment. "Uh huh."

The one time I'd shared these thoughts—these practical, albeit cynical, thoughts—Eilidh had given me the weirdest look. *But*, she'd said, *isn't that why we're still human? Treating our weak and sick with care?*

She'd said it like it was a good thing. Like it wasn't a stupid thing to cling to, like morals still matter after the world has ended. Like the Sunbathers had the wrong idea, somehow. I wasn't so sure about that.

They're all asleep in minutes while I lie awake, wondering how hot it might be above ground right now. I picture the sun caressing green summer leaves, the buzz of a bee flirting with each individual bright flower. The smell of fresh grass, of smoke and fire, of the salted sea, which I know to be not far from here, but which in the three years I've been living here I've never been able to witness. What I wouldn't give to stand barefoot on scorching sand, to feel the snarl of hot metal against my tender flesh.

Surrounded by steady, pungent breath, I compare our lives down here. The endless cold. The crumble of damp earth and pebbles under my back. The ceilings, propped up with narrow logs and splintered beams that could split under the slightest pressure. The smell of lingering memories, like the frilled, spongy underside of mushrooms. The dark steals more than sight; it steals our very selves. I wriggle out from Eilidh's embrace and creep back up the tunnel. Even thirty feet away, the brightness of the day stings my eyes. Outside, lavender bushes obscure the entrance, which provides us with some protection, but if they happened to step a certain way—

Two voices, nearby. I halt, my heart hammering, and press a hand over my chest as if that will stifle the noise. One laughs. They are often laughing, and why not? The Sunbathers are tanned and tall and beautiful. Their eyesight in daylight is better than perfect. Their strength is unparalleled. They are walking gods, illuminated by the eye of the paternal loving sun, while we scuttle around in the dirt and dark like vermin.

I creep a little closer. "Vic says they are close to finishing a great lamp like the one in Las Vegas, only better," one drawls. His voice reminds me of sunlight on snow—cold, crystalline, dangerous. "That one was forty-two point three billion candelas. A body could have gone stone-blind just looking at it too long. But this new lamp will be more powerful than that. More powerful than the Sun itself. Think of it, Cecily. Think how strong we shall be."

The second voice puts me in mind of a satisfied cat. Sleek. A single claw, currently sheathed. "And they say it will last?"

"They do."

I frown, not sure what they mean by *last*. I can't imagine something that bright—stronger than any stadium floodlight, more powerful than the sun. A desperate urge rises like bile; I want to stand in that light, stripped down to my bare skin, and let it take me. Their voices grow distant as they stroll away. The wind soughs in the trees, sliding between branches like a great invisible serpent, catching the cocked ear of every leaf, whispering ethereal temptations. I creep an inch closer, almost to the base of the steps. I want so badly to stick my head out, to taste the breeze, to win a single golden moment.

Instead, I retreat into the darkness like the lumbricine monster I am. A familiar thought drifts across my mind, a solo cloud in an otherwise baleful grey sky: *maybe if I was a Sunbather, I wouldn't hate myself quite so much.*

CHAPTER
TWO

Climate change had been a lot like seduction, in a way. Started slow, gradual, incremental changes over centuries as humans spread over the planet like spilled milk, turning everything we touched into rancid, sour wasteland. Not everything, of course, and not straight away, but sooner or later, we'd begun to notice our own effects on our surroundings. We'd blamed it on other people, other cultures. We'd claimed not to notice, claimed it was too subtle to tell for certain. Even when the overtures became more overt—bigger, more frequent storms, sea levels rising, salinity dropping, icebergs melting—we still brushed it off. Friendzoned the climate, told ourselves it wasn't real, that it was just a blip. No use getting overexcited and entering ourselves to amend the changes we'd wrought. That it would all return to normal soon.

Of course it didn't.

When the solar flares had worsened, turning into frequent and deadly bursts of intense radiation, most ordinary people had simply cowered, quaking, in their houses. When our special star was brightest, we tacked reflective foil over our windows to keep the worst of the sunshine out, and by the time the flares were happening every few days, rather than every few months, it seemed sensible to leave the foil up permanently. We grew used to living in reduced light, gaining a little relief from the shade of our homes.

Of course we did. We had no idea what was coming.

The first Sunbathers were ordinary people, with nothing to tie them together except a refusal to accept what was happening. A crowd of twenty or so had ignored the weather warnings and chosen to stay outside during a particularly bad solar flare. They'd chosen a tree-lined plaza, a patch of chartreuse grass just big enough to house each of their supine, mostly naked bodies. To begin with, they'd made a game of it, tunelessly belting a selection of appropriate songs including *Here Comes The Sun* and *This Little Light of Mine* and *Walking On Sunshine*. As their bodies changed—reddened, blackened, tanned, according to skin type, but all bubbling like molten cheese under a grill—they'd fallen silent. Several had deserted early on, fleeing for the safety of the shade. One had tried to withstand the pressure and, unable to drag himself to safety, had subsequently burst into agonized flames and died wailing. Several simply died where they lay, smoking like newly awoken volcanoes.

A photojournalist lying in wait in a first-floor office had captured the range of expressions of the still-living. A victorious snarl here, unfathomable grief there. Unusual countenances for people being burned alive, or so we thought. Most of them had cried, the tears steaming off their faces in hissing spurts. By the end of the flare, the daylight dimming to a more ordinary volume, every single still-living body was lit with a faint golden glow. They'd risen to their feet, graceful, but uncertain. One of them had leaned on a tree, cracking the trunk. They'd all stared. One of them had strutted across to a nearby lamppost. Had experimentally tugged. The lamppost had erupted from the ground in a shower of dirt and crumbled concrete, and the woman had held it uncertainly for a moment before raising it aloft like a trophy.

Afterwards, during a live interview, one of the group grinned into a waiting camera. "We met on a forum for people sick of living in fear," they said, their genitals blurred for the sake of the watching audience. "An anonymous source told us we'd been lied to about the danger of these flares. Glory in our sufferings!" they added, and the crowd chanted the words back in unison.

Behind them, the smoking corpses hissed and sputtered like guttering candles. Someone had blurred their genitals too, or at least, blurred where they thought the genitals might have been. "Sir? I wondered if you could tell me, uh, how did you know you wouldn't die?" the interviewer asked. Her thick makeup and glossy blonde curls couldn't distract from the fact that her hands were shaking and pale-knuckled around the offered mic.

"We didn't. We just accepted what the sun has to offer."

"Those who accept the sun will never die," another announced, standing side by side with the first. Their glow was ethereal, making the interviewer look washed out and haggard. A scruffy bird, surrounded by glittering specimens.

The interviewer cast a single glance towards the corpse before the mask of professional composure slipped back into place. "What makes you different from those of us inside?" she prompted.

Another cut in, "I don't think you should be asking what makes us different. I think you should be looking at what makes us the same. This could be you too," a glowing thumb, jabbed towards their heart, "if you do the work."

"Is it not..." the interviewer stumbled over her words, "uh, a dangerous procedure?"

As one, the crowd had stared at her; a great, golden Argus, many-limbed and hundred-eyed. "The sun's light shines on everyone. To hide in the darkness is to turn away the power and glory of the sun, who gives its warmth to aid us," the first person said decisively. "Why would you reject such a bountiful gift?"

"Some people are sensitive to the—" the interviewer began, but they interrupted her once more.

"Darkness is weakness. It's a sin. Aren't you tired of living in the shadows?" They turned to the camera, looking straight into the lens. "Step out and be seen."

After that, more than a thousand people braved the next flare. More than half of them survived it, and the idea grew roots, blossoming into something savage and bold. *The sun will burn away your frailties and leave you strong,* they insisted. *If you don't survive the process, it is your fault, not the sun's.* Those who had turned claimed they no longer indulged in vices, were no longer enticed by deviant bodily temptations. No more worrying and doubting and ruminating and deciding and discovering. The sun told them who they were, then burned the sins right out of their bodies and minds. They argued this was the apex of the human condition, adapted to our changing world instead of hiding from it in fear like animals.

Individual choice wasn't enough for the Sunbathers, though. We should have known that they wouldn't settle for notoriety. Spreading the message was only the start. They escalated gradually—recruitment evolved into pressurized solicitations, then into outright kidnappings. It wasn't enough that they had changed, that they were saved. They insisted on saving all of us too. If we resisted, that was merely proof that the darkness held us in sway. If we protested, then it was their obligation to perform their parts more aggressively, to rescue us from our own failings. They demanded loyalty and deference to the center of our universe above all else; a homage to the life-giving, vitalizing powers of the sun. Despite these tactics, many went willingly. Desperate to be cleansed, to be pure.

Growth happens in the dark too, Soph, Eilidh often reminds me. *Plenty of seeds require shade and cool conditions to thrive. The moon moves the tides. We need darkness as well as light for a circadian rhythm. Neither is better than the other. We simply are.*

Eilidh never asks if I am happy simply being. Maybe it never occurs to her to question it; maybe she knows she wouldn't like the answer.

SUNBATHERS

We sleep all day, caged in stuffy darkness. When finally a stream of cool air whispers down the tunnel, I'm already awake. I don't sleep well these days—not that I ever have. Eilidh, who has been snoring away peacefully for the last few hours, volunteers us both to go out again. It's an unnecessary announcement because we settled months ago on doing two-day shifts. Maya and Cygnet will go out tomorrow night and the one after; Old Jeff will sit on his dying arse and continue to stink while we spoonfeed him valuable nutrients. I bare my teeth in the dark while they fuss over him, though it's little release for my frustrations.

Eilidh's warm fingers slide along my shoulder, beckoning me outside. I follow her up the tunnel, dying for a piss and some fresh air. The moon is little more than a slit pupil, luminous and shy, and the air is still warm from the day's heat. The trees are full, and in the darkness impossible to tell that they're not the full green of early summer, but the crisp yellow of withering plants. The scene would be almost romantic... if it wasn't the end of the fucking world.

While I pee, Eilidh repeats her claim that she'd read a study, prior to the world ending, which concluded that Roque de los Muchachos Observatory—located in the Canary Islands—is the darkest place on Earth. She's told me the story many times, but the telling has grown more frequent of late. "We'll be safe there," she says, bending over to inspect something in the grass. "We'll be able to sleep under the stars, Soph. Won't that be wonderful?"

"Why not the Arctic? Or the Antarctic?" I can never remember which one is which. *Something to do with polar bears, maybe?* I wonder. The breeze is a warm throat, sighing the familiar scent of dry grass and sour sweat, but there's no trace of the Sunbathers I heard today. They smell different to everyone, at least everyone I've met post-apocalypse, but for me its distinctly lavender, a rounded, purple smell that threatens slumber whether you like it or not. I haven't told anyone what the Sunbathers said; knowledge is power, after all. It would only frighten them, and it's not as if we're in a position to do much about a threat anyway. Best we act like lonely fawns, low down in the grass. Still and dappled and silent. "One of the poles, anyway," I add. I have some idea that the days at the poles are dark more often than they're light. Maybe the cold, too, would keep away Sunbathers, who seem strongest in the warmth of eternal summer.

"That wouldn't work. In summer, the poles are basically daylight for twenty-four hours. It's like Sunbather paradise." Her mouth twitches downwards before curving back up into a smile. "Besides, I don't really fancy shagging in the snow. Do you?" She giggles. It's a terrible sound to come out of anyone over the age of three, and sends a ripple of rage through my fists, curling them like the dead leaves above us. "I'd much prefer warm sand, the roar of the ocean, the smell of coconuts. You, naked."

"Sounds good." I know she hopes for declarations, for me to indulge her stupid dreams and elaborate on them, but it's all I can do to tolerate the mention. No one is going anywhere, and hoping for anything like escape, freedom, or salvation, is just asking to be disappointed.

I pull her into a copse of trees—not that I expect anyone can see us in the darkness—and lean against a tree. Tugging my dusty shirt up and over my head, she nibbles her way down my neck, the tenderness of every bite turning my stomach. When her tongue circles my nipples, I'm dreaming of sunlight lapping on my skin. On her knees, she presses kisses along my bare thighs, nuzzles, and whispers *you smell so good baby* and *I love the way you taste* and *oh Soph, oh darling—*

Get on with it, I think, and roll my eyes while I push her face into my pussy.

She gets the message and laps eagerly. I never watch her eating me out. Even if it wasn't dark as hell, I'd rather not think of Eilidh. Instead, I picture what's-her-name with the freckles, who moved like a knife and had the devil's own tongue. I picture the girl who'd been my first sub, back in college, and the pretty little dog collar I'd made her polish before I spanked her so hard she hadn't been able to sit down in any of her classes. I picture the scarlet lips of an overgrown sun, ripe as a peach, fuzzy-fresh skin split, bursting, spilling raw yellow flesh into—

When I climax, it's the red glare of a summer afternoon I see behind my eyes, and I'm overcome with the urge to drive my knuckles into the sky, to claw and scratch and tear a ragged hole in that starry, velvet expanse. To fist the void of space until it begs for mercy.

"I love you, Soph," Eilidh whispers, while my aftershocks ripple through me, making it hard to stay standing.

For once, I'm glad of the darkness. She can't see the wince, can't see the way my throat bobs as I swallow hard. Can't watch my eyes blink back post-coital tears. She doesn't declare her love often; she knows I don't like it. I haven't said it back, not even once. I was in danger of doing it, four months ago, but the fling I had with what's-her-name helped put a necessary barrier between me and the words. Real love isn't grubbing around in the darkness, taking whatever scraps you can, no matter how my chest buzzes when Eilidh kisses me.

It's not real, I tell myself. *It can't possibly be real.*

I almost believe myself.

CHAPTER
THREE

We do a quick recon, swinging out in a wide, westward arc from the mouth of the burrow. We have maybe five hours of darkness before the sun begins to rise; it's a decent chunk of time compared to what it'll be like in high summer, when we'll spend twenty-three hours every day in our dank little wormhole and only venture out for one measly hour. Even then, our safety isn't guaranteed. The Sunbathers are imbued with super-human strength and senses, making them difficult predators to avoid completely, though from what I've seen, they're not any smarter than us. If anything, maybe they're a little stupider, or maybe it just seems that way because of their absolute belief in their solar doctrine. It's not the religion part that bothers me, really; it's just that I've never personally been that certain of anything.

Our recons usually entail a wide sweep of the area to make sure there are no traces of Sunbathers—campfires left over from the daytime, towels imprinted with crime-scene-outlines of their blood-brown sweat, reflective foils which they use during cloudy periods to enhance every single possible unit of luminescence. The cloudy days are, at least from my snatched glimpses, less frequent than they were two years ago. In another two, they might be absent entirely. The thought has burrowed into my mind like an ingrown hair, has grown an itchy red pimple of fear around it. A day will come when there won't be any more clouds. And soon after that, a day might come when night never falls, when nothing is ever truly dark again. It's not a question of *if*, but *when*.

"Soph?" Eilidh whispers, and I shake myself from my reverie.

She offers me a water bottle. I take it and gulp down the tepid, saliva-warm liquid. The cache of water bottles is a constant conundrum, since they need to be in direct sunlight to kill bacteria, but not out in the open in case they're spotted by Sunbathers. It would be a total giveaway that there are humans nearby, and they're not exactly the type to let sleeping dogs lie.

We fall into our usual walking pattern. Eilidh watches our left, while I watch our right. No Sunbather could possibly be out in such darkness, but rival gangs of humans are sometimes desperate. We turn on each other in times of danger—it's just another thing that sets us apart from them. I've never seen a Sunbather fight another Sunbather, not for food or light or status, though what they do in the confines of their own little city-states is a mystery to us. In the distance, a Sunbather camp lights up the night sky like a rave. Strobe lights flicker and flash in a rainbow of whites and creams, slashing the underside of clouds with a thousand unnoticed cuts. I've heard they sleep cocooned inside individual tanning beds, swaddled in light. A single shadow won't phase them, and a dim room would simply inflict a high degree of pain. Death for a Sunbather requires full darkness; they have the advantage over us in this respect since it's much easier to drag a body out of a hole than it is to drag them in. We tried, once, and lost four members of our community in the struggle.

Too bad none of them were Old Jeff.

When Eilidh takes my hand I let her, even though it broadcasts weakness, ripe for the picking. The copse of trees ranges another half-mile, and then it's all open ground. We plod over still-warm soil, soft and crumbling under our boots, and climb over an old stone wall that was probably built by farmhands hundreds of years ago, back when the sun was still something to be enjoyed and treasured. This whole area used to be farms, surrounding a nice little suburb, though I haven't seen a single living cow or sheep in over a year. The city, ten miles further west, is pretty much deserted now. I sigh. I'd kill for a single hour inside my old apartment: my galley kitchen, my tiny bedroom with the sloping ceiling. I even miss the neighbours' stupid cat, who used to risk his neck jumping a four-foot gap to my Juliette balcony just to piss all over my basil plants.

After the first Sunbathers turned, it took six months before things really kicked off. Change had been happening gradually, of course, but the turning point was a big corporate building in the middle of the city called Riverside Plaza. I still don't know why it started, or who picked it as a target—or whether it was chosen to make a point, or was simply the result of pure coincidence—but one morning, Sunbathers started smashing the glass windows on the ground floor. Some of them braved the lobby inside to drag out four security guards. Two fought and were beaten to death. Two submitted to the Burn. One made it out alive and was carried off triumphantly by the horde. The next day, in the course of admiring his new body, the recently-turned security guard returned, heading up a frothing mass of perfect flesh. He used his new power to scale the building, smashing every window he could reach.

We'd thought houses and buildings were safe zones, as Sunbathers couldn't enter comfortably. The artificial lighting we'd used for a hundred years didn't do anything for them, so it was like entering a dim room—painful, though not impossible. We'd underestimated their anger, their determination, their fervor. Dozens died in the attack on Riverside and hundreds more in the riots that followed. Under the cover of night, humans raided Sunbather camps, dragging them from their tanning beds, killing them with darkness. Videos of these nocturnal battles were shaky and grainy at best, but it was clear that darkness was their weakness.

A Sunbather drenched in darkness would last only a minute at most, the golden glow receding until the skin reflected only a kind of milky negative. Their blood ran luminous white, thick as cream, pouring from their ears, eyes, and mouths. Infuriated by these attacks and by the way humans kept retreating into the comfort zones of walled buildings during the day, like snails shrinking back into the safe confines of their shells, the Sunbathers began to rip away the walls and roofs of everything they could find. Once they were able to expose the tender, cowering humans inside, they'd pull them out, strip them naked, throw them into the sun, and let them burn.

It was a small step from hunting us for sport to hunting us for real. Some say we did it to ourselves, that if we hadn't fought back then they would have left us alone eventually. I know that isn't true. From the very beginning, the Sunbathers had wanted to turn everybody in the world. That was what they said on TV and on the radio, their parroted talking point. Now, two years after the Burn, anyone who hasn't chosen to endure the trial by sunshine is automatically a friend of the dark.

That's what they call us, among much else: friend of the dark, moon-lovers, goddamn worms.

We should have seen it coming. Those who have changed and adapted consider themselves higher on the branches of the tree of life. The Sunbathers are ahead, and we didn't jump on the bandwagon while we had a chance. Some of us were too afraid, some too stubborn. Either way, we're traitors to them. And treason, in all places at all times, comes with only one punishment.

Death.

BY THE TIME I start to smell the sea, it's time to turn back. I've wanted to see it for so long, even in darkness, but it's too much of a risk. Eilidh would prefer our burrow to be further away, but the soil precludes digging in a lot of places. Old, abandoned mines might look helpful but they're the first place any group of terrified humans would think to flee, and besides, they're too well-charted on maps.

We head a half-mile south, picking up a few handfuls of berries on the way, then begin the long trek back. The stars are twinkling, the sky a deep navy slashed with lighter streaks of blue, as if there's a rich vein of sapphires running through it. I vaguely remember some news article about a planet where it rained diamonds and am trying to recall which one when Eilidh squeezes my hand hard enough to make my knuckles crack. We halt instantly. I bite back a yelp and scan the area. It only takes me a moment to clock what she's already seen—the remains of a campfire, on the outskirts of a group of trees. She lets go of my hand and we head for it. Though I know we're safe in the darkness, my senses are on high alert. The flutter of a bird on a nearby branch sends my pulse skyrocketing. The smell of charred meat wafting from the campfire makes my mouth water.

An ember blinks at us, a single red eye descending into permanent slumber. I stare down at the trampled grass, the imprint of bare feet in the ashes. There were at least four Sunbathers, maybe more. I swallow, and turn over a roughly-hewn log with my boot, only to find it's not a log at all. One breast is still visible, the flesh scored deeply around it. "Shit."

"Oh god." Eilidh claps a hand over her mouth and backs away.

I shrug. I've witnessed far worse, unfortunately. "It's nothing we haven't seen before."

She glares at me reproachfully. "It's not like I ever get used to it. That was once a person, Soph."

Who cares? I think. *Just be glad it's not us.*

"This is too close." She's transitioned to biting her thumbnail. "We're not even a mile from home. And it wasn't there four days ago when Cygnet and Maya did their recon."

She's right. It's not good news. "Yeah."

Eilidh darts forward and clings to me. I pat her back, smooth down her hair, and wonder how I can steal just a single bite of the meat without her noticing. We stand there for long minutes while she weeps quietly into my shoulder, and all I can think of is my teeth sinking into her neck. The skin giving way. The blood, spurting and hot. The relief of flesh, solid and simple, lining my belly.

I don't get a chance to act out my fantasy. She insists we search every inch of the campsite for clues and then the surrounding area. We find more evidence of Sunbathers: a gnawed ulna tossed into the grass, already covered by industrious ants. A mess of scarlet gloop that might have once been organs. A carafe of something potent that stinks of fermentation. A shredded t-shirt, yellowed with age and sweat and grime. A pair of walking shoes, thick-heeled and sturdy. It's confirmation of what we already know, since only we wear clothes, only we feel shame. Sunbathers are past all that. They're elevated. Superior. Worthier.

WE HASTEN back to the burrow, where Eilidh tells the group everything. "We need a plan," she announces.

"Hold on," Maya's voice is a bowstring, taut with expectation. "We should check it out for the next couple of days to see if it's a repeated thing. They might just be moving through. Some of them do. It wouldn't be the first time."

Cygnet clears their throat. "Where is camp?"

"West, less than a mile," Eilidh says. "Not far from the stream."

Maya clicks impatiently. "One of you should come to show us the way. We can't afford to waste any time."

Eilidh hesitates. "I'll go," I offer. "You stay and rest. I know how much it upsets you."

Her fingers find mine in the darkness. "Thanks," she breathes, and I roll my shoulders, embarrassed, though it's not as if she can see me.

When the endless chatter dies down, and we're left with only our grumbling bellies to sing us to sleep, I slide my hand between my legs and think again of the torso, picture the sole remaining breast, the soft curve of the abdomen. I stifle a groan with one hand, teasing my hole with the other until I can't bear it any longer, drawing rough, shaky circles into deepening wetness, never quite giving myself what I need. Eilidh's arm brushes my side as she turns, her breath stuttering before it evens out again. Wincing, I inch away, needing to be untouched in this moment as I picture the headless torso alive and writhing under me. The taupe-sweat-stink of my group is replaced by the acrid, heady smell of charred animal, red as carmine, tart as unripe cherries. My hips buck against my hand desperately, my heels pushing into the dirt to gain the slightest purchase. I need more—not a head, not a face, but more. Maybe there's a bone I didn't see jutting out below the bellybutton, maybe a fragment of pelvic girdle already lubricated with blood, just enough to give a little friction while I finally, blessedly, press my lips against warm, life-giving flesh, snarling with pleasure, rutting hard, and tear a whole mouthful of meat off and clamp down on more and more, filling my mouth with so much meat I can hardly breathe and—

 I come so hard my teeth break the skin of my left hand.

CHAPTER
FOUR

I sleep well and deeply, though when I wake up everyone but Maya is still firmly gripped in slumber's sweaty fist. I know it's Maya because she clicks to herself, a strange combination of tongue and teeth which form a nonsensical string of morse code. I spider-crawl over Eilidh's prone body, making sure I don't step on her, and creep back up the tunnel, stopping about twenty feet from the entrance to settle myself on the packed dirt. The breeze—what little I can feel of it—is blissfully tepid against my face after the cool of the burrow, and in the gloaming, the stars are mere blood speckles spattered around the raw orange wound of the sky.

It's likely that the Sunbathers I eavesdropped on two days ago were the ones who'd made the nearby campfire. I still haven't told the others what I overheard them talking about, though I've been wondering about it ever since. I lean back against the wall of the tunnel and shake my head, frustration prickling between my shoulder blades. It makes no sense; what the hell kind of use would a lamp be to a Sunbather? Only the sun can sustain them; at least, as far as any of us know. Still, something keeps tickling the back of my mind. An idea, unremembered. I chew on a fingernail, tasting salt and grime. Is it possible that they've found a way to harness the sun? Could they catch it and store it and turn it into some kind of light without losing any element of that original sunshine? If so, we're royally screwed. They'd be able to get at us anywhere, any time. We'd all be as good as dead.

Eilidh joins me when the twilight falls, and though she tries to drum up conversation, I'm in no mood to be charitable. She eventually leaves me alone, though insists on hugging me tightly before she heads back down to the burrow. She probably thinks I resent her for having to go out again, but any time spent away from the pervasive stench of Old Jeff's foul, rotten foot is a relief.

As promised, I wait for Cygnet and Maya. We take a little time in the privacy of the trees, evacuating our bladder or bowels as necessary, and when the sky becomes the shade I would never dream of describing out loud as *chambray*, we finally leave. Neither of them are incautious people, but their impatience to see what we've seen is palpable. A sliver of infant moon peeks between curtains of cloud, spying on us as we set off in the right direction. They fall into stride beside me, silent and serious, and we walk for almost a half-mile until we get to the outskirts of the grove of trees. The campsite is still there, and before we even get close I already know the Sunbathers have been back to it today. The grass is patchy with dark smears of blood, and the torso from the day before is nowhere to be seen. I don't think they'd have eaten it, not the day after. They seem to prefer their food fresh. Wriggling. One of them probably chucked it into the bushes where it'll feed a den of furry rodents for a week. *Fucking waste*, I think.

Maya bends and touches the ashes of the campfire with a single finger. "Still warm. Not hot, but warm. They definitely used it today." She stands, sighs, and wipes her hands on her dark jeans. Raw denim, she'd called it. Funny what used to matter to us: fashion, politics, internet discourse.

"It might be a roving group, like you said," I point out.

"Two nights isn't really enough to form any kind of real conclusion." Maya runs a hand over her black, twisted braids. The mole under her left eye, as brown as the iris itself, looks bigger than I remember. Maybe it's just a trick of the light, what little there is. "We don't know if they used it for a day or two before you found it, or whether that was the first time. We can't know if they intend to stick around." She sighs again. "But it's a bad sign."

Cygnet frowns and scratches their chin. They were always skinny, but lately they've begun to look gaunt, the grey around their temples spreading, their once close-cropped hair turning shaggy and unkempt. Even their sweater—grey, woollen, plucked off a bloodless body a couple of months ago—has begun to unravel at the hems, making it look less hipster-cosy and more unhoused-veteran-abandoned-by-country. "We change? Change, uh, house?"

I bite back a bitter laugh. Our burrow is as far from a house as it could possibly be. I can still vividly picture my old apartment, with all the luxuries I treasured—a stove-top cafetière, the latest gaming console, abstract artwork hanging on every wall—and my laugh threatens to turn into a sob. These days I'd happily settle for the most basic amenities: a flushing toilet, a working oven, a single hot shower.

"Maybe," Maya pats Cygnet on the shoulder. "We need to take a vote first. Group decision, yeah?"

I turn away so that neither of them see my rolled eyes and busy myself looking for any scraps of food the careless Sunbathers left behind. We gather up whatever we can find: several more peaches, bruised but edible. A few forgotten, ashy eggs that have probably been roasted of every drop of internal moisture but at least they're valuable protein. A half-stripped haunch that came from something bovine, not human, hangs from a nearby tree branch. Maya—a self-professed vegetarian—hangs back while Cygnet stoops and sniffs it.

"Poison," they announce, wrinkling their nose.

Disappointment is a shiny penny under my tongue, coppery and bitter. "How can you tell?"

They beckon me over. "Smell."

I obey, reluctantly. The aroma is faint and familiar, though I haven't smelled it in a long, long time. "What's that? Garlic?"

"Yes, but no." They shake their head. "Uh…" their fingers wave in the air as if conducting an invisible orchestra. "When make sword? Yes?"

Maya and I stare at them, baffled. Cygnet blinks and tries again. "Hot metal." They mime pouring something and then perform a hammering action. "Hot place. Hit the metal. You know?"

"Smelting?" Maya guesses. "Like a blacksmith?"

"Yes, but… more big."

I frown. "Like a factory? Or a mine?" I'm not really following whatever it is they're trying to explain, but I do my best. "Are you saying the Sunbathers put metal in the meat?"

Cygnet shakes their head, exasperated.

"Arsenic," Maya breathes. "They've laced it with arsenic."

That seems like a wild leap of logic to me. "What? How the hell—"

"It's a byproduct of smelting," she says, as if that's a totally normal thing to know. "You can also obtain it from natural resources, though I'd be willing to bet my life that no Sunbathers has ever sullied their hands with anything remotely agricultural. And that makes for problem number two, as if them setting traps wasn't bad enough. If they're smelting, they're mining somehow."

"They can't mine," I point out, unable to keep a snide edge from my voice. "In case you forgot, there aren't exactly a lot of open air mines around here."

"Well, at the very least they're gathering something in large quantities. Why would they do something like that?"

"To make," Cygnet supplies, doing the hammering action again. "To build."

The feeling in my stomach is a witch's cauldron, bubbling and sour and neon green. I know exactly what they're building, though I don't know why. I open my mouth to say something, though I hardly know what, but Maya interrupts me.

"God, they're sick." She's pointing at the campfire, at something spitted that looks suspiciously like a skinned, handless arm. If I squint, I could easily mistake it for a beef round. My mouth begins to water. Instinctively, I reach for the meat, but she slaps my hands away. "What the fuck are you doing?"

"We could use the protein," I say, a vein in my temple suddenly throbbing. I want to snarl, to leap on her and fight in the dirt like a dog, to scruff her until she submits to me.

"That's not funny." She stares at me, but I don't back down. "Sophie, really, we're not so desperate that we—"

"I'm fucking starving, okay? Christ, get off my back. Besides, they won't expect us to take this, so they wouldn't have poisoned it. Here," I lift the cut of meat and offer it to Cygnet, who at least doesn't balk. "Tell me—does this smell like anything?"

They sniff. "No. Safe."

"See?"

Maya's hands are on her hips, her eyes bright with angry tears. "You've got to be kidding. I can't believe that you would even consider—"

"I'm taking it, okay?" I sigh. "It's for me and whoever else wants some. No one's force-feeding you, so don't get your knickers in a bloody twist about it."

"Bitch!" she snaps and stomps off, swinging the bag of peaches as she goes.

Cygnet shrugs and follows, leaving me to bring up the rear. I unhook the arm and carry it over my shoulder. The scent of the meat, fatty and rich, wafts towards me. I swallow down drool, coming so fast and thick that it almost chokes me, and leaves me spluttering. I've done plenty of ugly things in order to survive. Honestly, consuming human flesh doesn't seem so bad compared to some of the others. The stories we tell ourselves to stay alive are the worst nightmares of all.

When I can't bear it any longer, I take a tentative bite of the arm. It's everything I hoped and also, nothing at all like I'd expected; pork with a slightly bitter aftertaste. I gag but keep chewing until the desire to retch abates. Several more bites sustain me on the march—clearly we're not going back to the burrow just yet, as Maya has veered east. I'd thought she was going to run straight back so she could snitch on me to Eilidh, but apparently we're doing a whole recon. *Whatever.* She can seethe as much as she wants, but it's too late. I've already eaten the most forbidden fruit.

Cygnet's lanky figure lopes ahead of me, their long legs eating up the ground. I can no longer see Maya, who must have ducked off the path somewhere. A bird takes flight from a tree thirty feet ahead, and I stare in that direction, my jaws still working, a slurry of masticated arm-meat sloshing around in my mouth. Maya appears from behind a clump of bushes, empty-handed and anguished. "They found our water," she whispers, voice bright with unshed tears. "How did they —Shit. It's all gone."

In disbelief, I push past her and check behind the bushes. The ground is littered with empty plastic bottles. The lids have been unscrewed, the precious contents dumped onto the thirsty ground. I let loose a string of creative curses and aim a kick at the nearest tree. We have three more supply spots but even so, my chest is banded with sudden, tight certainty. If the Sunbathers found this one, they probably went looking for the others too. Without a safe place to purify water, we're screwed. We'd only last a couple of days without it, and drinking straight from the stream will have us shitting our guts out, worsening the dehydration. Hastening our demise.

I'd scoffed at Cygnet's question of whether we should move, whether the Sunbathers were too close, but they'd been totally right. After discovering this cache, the Sunbathers would know for sure there was a skulk of us nearby. It was simply a matter of time before they decided to root us out.

CHAPTER
FIVE

Back in the burrow, the news about the campsite is met with horrified silence. Old Jeff shifts, and I can tell by the way air whistles through his nose that his sinuses are swelling, that he's on the verge of tears if not crying already. There's no way he can walk on his wounded foot, so if the rest of us agree to leave, we'll have to leave him behind. He might find some mercy with the group who live in the other burrow, but I doubt it; there was dissension in the ranks even before what's-her-name-with-the-freckles died, and though we never talked about such things, I got the impression she was someone people would obey, or at least follow. The only other people I've seen scuttling into that burrow are two teen girls and a man in his early twenties. Not exactly a harem, but probably reasonably close-knit, if they've stuck together this long. Who the hell would willingly take on the responsibility of feeding and caring for some old man they don't even know?

I frown into the darkness. I don't even know how aged Old Jeff is. I try to picture the last time I saw him by faint starlight, but there's only a vague impression of wrinkled jowls and a shiny, bald head. Definitely old enough to be a liability, though he could be useful bait.

"No worry," Cygnet says, rustling on my left. Patting Old Jeff, probably, like a dog who's scared of a thunderstorm.

Maya, who thankfully seems to have forgotten about my brief foray into cannibalism, clicks her tongue against her teeth. "We're all in this together, okay? It's what sets us apart from the Sunbathers. We have community."

Christ, I think. *Community isn't going to stop us from being ripped apart like baby bunnies when the wolf slides into our warren. As if the Sunbathers don't also have community.* Maybe this is a human thing, to be pointlessly, stupidly optimistic in the face of clear and present danger.

"Maybe this is a sign," Eilidh chimes in. "I just think... Look, I know I've said this before, but maybe we should head for the Canary Islands."

I wince. She can't help herself. She knows it means making sacrifices, but she wants it so badly she's entertaining the notion of breaking the group bonds, maybe even leaving the others behind if it means reaching her goal. An unexpected wave of sympathy twangs in my chest. Maybe we're a little more alike than I thought.

"And what happens," Maya asks, "when we get to a place where no one has dug burrows? Where will we sleep then?"

"There are cave systems along the coast," Eilidh insists. "Abandoned mines. Probably boats too, if we can get to the harbour before dawn breaks. Like, I don't know, yachts and stuff. Even a ferry would do. My dad used to have a boat so I know how to—"

"You're delusional if you think that's ever going to work." Maya clicks again; the smallest sound of teeth, scraping over cracked lips. Irritation has finally spilled into her voice, pooling dark and hot. She's trying not to add something else, trying not to cross a line by making accusations she can't rescind. "You think they won't notice? That they haven't locked up everything that we could use to escape? That they haven't laid traps or whatever?"

"But once we're out on open ocean, we're safe," Eilidh persists. "It's not as if they can take their tanning beds onto a boat, so—"

"They swim," Cygnet interrupts.

Maya sighs. "Exactly. And they go a lot faster than you think." A slight hesitation. "I've seen them do it. Pull people off boats and hold them underwater. They laughed until the bubbles stopped, and then they—" She clears her throat. "Well, suffice to say they gutted them like fish. There's no fucking way I'm going anywhere near the coast."

"You saw the campfire." Eilidh's voice is angrier than I've ever heard it. "You know how close it is. So what's your plan, then, huh? We sit here and hope they don't notice us? We need to go, Maya. Can we at least agree on that, even if we don't agree on where—"

"And what about Jeff?" Maya says, changing tack. A dirty trick, which I mentally applaud.

"Don't you worry about me, girls. I'll be fine." He's definitely crying.

Christ, I'm so bored of this conversation. I lean against the dirt wall and chew a fingernail. My hands stink of grease and ashes, and the meat which had seemed so delicious and necessary before is churning uncomfortably in my stomach. I don't know why they bother to try to convince each other. *People who want to go, should go. People who want to stay, should stay. There. Sorted.* It doesn't have to be an endless argument about who and where and what's the most ethical, noble thing to do. Besides, I'm not even sure I believe in morality anymore. The Sunbathers must possess something we don't, some reason or essential characteristic that explains why they were spared, why each surviving person was deemed strong or worthy enough to live through the Burn. A Sunbather would never bother arguing to save a wounded old man. They're the ultimate predator, clean and decisive. Not for the first time, I wonder what it would be like to be that free of indecision, of doubt, of qualms. It must feel bloody amazing.

"We should vote on it," Maya announces.

"Soph?" Eilidh's fingers find my arm and squeeze. "What do you think?"

"I vote to go." I shrug. "Sorry, pal. It is what it is."

Old Jeff whimpers. Maya clicks. "I vote to stay," she says.

Of course you do. "I vote go. I help Jeff when walk." Cygnet sounds so sure, but the guy is two hundred pounds of dead weight. I give them half a mile before it becomes obvious that he's completely fucked, and in being so fucked, fucks us all in turn.

"I vote to go. Obviously, we'll all try to help Jeff, that's not even a question." Eilidh's fingers slide down and find my hand, but I shake her off. I'm so damn tired of listening to them fret and whine and try to avoid accepting reality. This insistence on compassion is going to get us all killed, which is actually the least compassionate choice of all, in the grand state of things.

I scramble out into the tunnel, ignoring the whiny way Eilidh calls my name. "Leave her be," Maya snaps. "For God's sake, Eilidh, get a grip."

The instruction evidently has an effect, since no one follows me into the tunnel. Dawn is only just breaking—I can see pale light dribbling down through the entrance—and I can't help myself. I scuttle closer. A breeze billows down, stroking my skin with a thousand breath-warm feathers. Closer. The scent of lavender wafts towards me. Closer. No one is around to stop me. Why shouldn't I indulge everything I desire for a single shining moment? Anyway, if we left the burrow we'd have to risk being in the open air during the day, possibly for hours at a time, and therefore it's actually good to test it out now, and now my foot is on the bottom earthen stair and I am raising myself up, up, until my head is above ground, my eyes stinging with the delicious pain of overwhelming light and I want to wail as if I've just been birthed into a strange new world, bloody and new, and—

A Sunbather grabs me by the throat and hauls me upwards. Panicked, I splutter, clawing at her fingers, but she takes no more notice than if I were an flitting butterfly. Her dark hair is streaked with grey, her skin a luminous tan. Her eyes are a dazzling, vulpine amber. Her naked body is sculpted to perfection, every sinew and muscle on show, cocooned in a soft layer of womanflesh. She's a god. She's beauty, personified.

And she's going to murder me.

"Look," she says, and I recognise her voice from the other day; calm, collected, predatory. *Cecily*, he called her. My feet dangle inches from the ground, my vision turning red at the edges as she turns, carrying me in front of her as if I were a particularly disgusting bag of garbage. My chest is on fire, my treacherous bodily weight pulling me down, choking me further. *This is it*, I think, *this is how my world ends*. "Another worm, just where I predicted it would be. What do you think, Jacob?" Her top lip twitches into a snarl. "Shall I make it stop wriggling?"

CHAPTER
SIX

I claw at her hand, scrabbling, my feet trying to gain purchase on air. There's a flicker in my peripheral vision as her companion approaches, frowning. His eyes are a pale, bleached blue; a violent, beautiful contrast to his dark skin. His thighs are thick and muscular. His collarbones are two thick boughs pulled taut above smooth pecs. "You have such a talent for the hunt, sister."

She hums appreciatively, though her eyes never leave my face.

"I want—" I choke. "I want—" I don't know why I expect her hand to loosen, but it doesn't. *They're merciless*, I remind myself. It's what I admired about them. "—to be one of you," I wheeze.

I hadn't exactly planned to say it, but even as the words come out I hear the truth in them. Her grip slackens a little, just enough for me to draw a single breath and cough it out. I gasp, my throat throbbing with blue-hot pain. It feels like I imagine being hanged would, though I doubt anyone ever fancied their noose before.

"We love to hear those words, don't we, brother?" Her snarl fades, though her hand doesn't waver. The Sunbathers exchange looks; his hands flash rapidly, signally some complicated pattern I can't possibly parse. "Hmm." She turns back to me, and lowers me until my tiptoes touch solid earth, then lets go and steps back. "Some would rather die than join us. What makes you different?"

"I, uh— I don't know." I massage my aching throat, watching her for any sudden movements. Fear roots me to the ground, as steady as any tree. Despite the already oppressive heat of the day, my hands are icy with terror. I could lunge backwards, hurl myself back into the burrow, run and warn the others, but that would only put them in danger too. Plus, she'd catch me long before I reached it; her speed and reflexes far outshine my own. At least, that's how I justify remaining still. It's nothing to do with the fact that now I'm actually in front of them, I'm confronted with the real, flesh-and-blood evidence of my own failings. She's right, I am a worm. In the bright light of day, no lie about equality can exist. "But please believe me, I want to," I add, sweat dribbling down my spine. "I'll do it. I'll do it right now, right this second."

"The ritual kills many more than it saves, these days. You've left it rather late, worm." The male Sunbather—Jacob—studies me. Takes in the appalling state of my clothing, my pale skin, the way I can hardly bear to open my eyes even in this dull light. The sunlight picks out the hollow of his cheekbones, deep enough to bury a soul. "Still, even trying should absolve you somewhat. We don't often turn a soul away who begs to be saved."

I nod vigorously. *So magnanimous.* They're right, of course; I'm nothing compared to them. I fall to my knees and babble a stream of nonsensical pleading, telling them how beautiful they are, confessing how disgusting I am, how weak. They tolerate this for a minute or two, their smiles placid. Another bout of hand-waving passes between them. Cecily shrugs and turns away, face upturned to the sun. Her right ear is pointing in the direction of the entrance to the burrow, only twenty feet away, and though I can't hear anything, I know her senses are much keener than mine.

"Before you can undergo the Burn, we must prepare you."

My heart is hammering so hard I feel like I'm going to faint. I didn't know that there was anything else to it other than the sun part.

Is this a new thing? Are they playing with me right before they kill me? There's no way to tell, so I nod again, trying to look as obedient and un-wormy as possible.

"The induction needs blood for the ritual," he continues.

Still kneeling, I bow my head and hold out my arms to await the cuts or bites that are surely coming. "Not your own blood," Cecily says. "A proper sacrifice goes much deeper than blood or bone. You must show your devotion."

"To the sun?" I ask, uncertain.

"To yourself. To the Path." She pronounces the last word oddly, as if it's important enough to capitalise. "You have to renounce the darkness. Cast off your sins. Sear away the taint of your old ways. Kill what you love most, what has tied you to the darkness for so long. Only then can you be ready to receive the blessing. Only then will the Burn spare you and grant you the greatest powers of all."

What's my alternative, really—becoming another spitted limb strung across a campfire like what's-her-name? *Screw that.*

Jacob bends down, grabs my chin and raises my eyes to meet his. "Tell us about your little wormhole," he purrs. "How far does it extend? How deep? How many little worms tangle together in the darkness?"

I can hardly spill the secret fast enough. I tell them how the burrow splits, how it whorls under the pockmarked land, how our little patch is laid out and how I've never been inside the other tunnel. I tell them about our group, about Old Jeff's foot, about the other group in the other tunnel. I tell them anything and everything in the hopes that the sum total of my confessions will be equal to the value of my life.

He lets go of my chin and stands, stretches godlike before me, muscles rippling crow-blue-black in the sunshine. My face is wet and my eyes sting, though I can't tell if it's from the strain of the light or fear or both. I'd thought I was beyond this kind of existential terror, and although dying by Sunbather would be an honor, I'd still rather live. Every breath I suck down through my bruised windpipe is another moment alive. I never appreciated that before, was always too shitty and cynical to relish sentience.

All that will change now. It has to change.

"Pick a sacrifice," Jacob says. "Life requires death."

"And godhood requires giving up one's humanity," Cecily adds.

Not mortality, I notice, *but humanity*. It's a trolley problem, then—either I choose at least one person to die as my sacrifice, or my entire group dies one by one. Simple, really. I make a half-hearted plan to talk Old Jeff into coming with me; who'd miss him, after all? The idea fizzles out before I get more than a couple of steps in. The truth is only one person is connecting me to the darkness, who'd ever made me feel even remotely okay about being there.

They watch my face keenly, watch the realization dawning. Pleasure ripens in their knife-eyes and blooms on their scythe-lips. "We'll wait here. Hurry. Bring your lamb."

I stumble back towards the burrow and descend. My vision dances with sunspots, floating like pale amoeba against the petri dish of the darkness. Nausea simmers in my stomach; I bite down hard on my hand, letting the pain ground me. If I don't do this, they'll root the rest of us out anyway. This way, I can at least save myself.

Eilidh is waiting for me at the entrance to the den. "Where the hell were you?" she whispers. "I called, but you didn't—"

The words slide out, easier than they should. "I found something topside. Come and see."

"Soph, you know it's not safe," she protests.

I lean into her, rest my temple against the groove of her neck, press my nose into the hollow there, and feel her pulse skitter. "Please," I say. "Please just do this one thing for me and I'll never ask you for anything ever again."

She hesitates.

I pitch my voice low, warm, human for the last time. "I love you."

It's enough. Her fingers slide into mine and I squeeze, feeling her sharp bones, her callouses, all the fortune-told lines criss-crossing her sweaty palm.

The Sunbathers catch her on the outskirts of the grove. "Soph!" she screams. "Soph, run!" The third time, my name is halved by suspicion.

I turn away from the betrayal, not wanting to see her last moments. A quick cut, they said. A sharp twist, they said. The wound would heal soon enough; for me, anyway. A faint gurgle behind me informs me that the deed is done. I lift my face to the sky—oh, the blue sky!—and position myself like a flower, arms outstretched. I want to throw up, to purge myself inside as well as out, but I swallow the urge down, afraid to sully the moment. The sound of dragging—a heavy, leaden slither—could be anything.

Not necessarily a body.

Not necessarily my fault.

My body is racked with dry sobs. I twitch helplessly as the Sunbathers strip me of my clothing, leaving me entirely exposed. I don't fight it or help them, but simply lie there, staring up at a single cloud. The sky is a lambent, aquamarine flame, the sun a white, coruscating radiance. I wonder how I look through Sunbather eyes—a pale disgusting worm, thrashing alone on the dry ground. *No matter*, I think. In a couple of minutes, I'll be dead or one of them. I pray for the latter, though I don't know who would bother listening to me, not after what I just did.

The Sunbathers order me to spread my limbs like a star. I comply, dragging myself into the right shape, the soil already uncomfortably warm under my skin. They wait in silence and so do I, listening to the sound of their breathing until the sun has risen a little higher. I'd thought it might need to be at its zenith—high noon seemed appropriately dramatic, but it can't be more than ten o'clock when my skin begins to blister. I remember sunshine from my childhood as a pleasant warmth, from my teenage years as a baking roast, from my twenties as an ever-present blaze. I'd thought my memories were relatively intact, but I don't remember anything ever being as bad as this.

I howl as the sun's rays sear my skin. The smell of my sizzling flesh, pork-rich and crackling deliciously, is sickening. I turn my head to vomit but there's no time—the red glare becomes a white-hot scald over my whole body, interspersed with the pop-pop-pop of tiny blisters bursting along my bare stomach like simmering water, and I open my mouth as the sunshine coats me, covers me, fills me up, and I scream as if by emptying my lungs I might drown myself all the faster, and—

My world is full of searing, ferocious pain. Time roars by in a torrent, washing my senses away, boiling them clean. *I am dying I am dying I am more alive than I have ever been*

I am dead

I am dead or alive or both

I am not I am not I am not I am

I didn't know I didn't know that it would feel so

stop go on stop let it end please oh jesus fuck let it be over let me die

When it finally ends, I lie dazed and whimpering. "Hmm. She might need a second round," Jacob says, stroking his bare chin.

My cracked eyelids flicker. *Please, no more.* Cecily shrugs and tosses her beautiful mane over her shoulder. "We must endure the heat to stand in the light. Is that not so?"

"Of course, sister," he agrees.

I reach out, pawing at the air, desperate for any scrap of comfort, any atom of reassurance. *Please,* I silently mouth. *Please. Help me.*

They instantly retreat. "Every soul stands alone," Jacob says. His voice is a mirrored lake, glassy and pure, but a muscle jumps in his jaw and belies his displeasure. "Needless touching is a vice we do not indulge in, unless it's your Chosen One, or you're inflicting necessary pain on worms. You have much to learn, new sister."

Stricken, I let my hand flop onto the dirt. Yellow grass crunches under their footsteps as they stroll away, leaving me alone and in agony. I crane my head, hissing at the pain, and stare down at my body. My skin is rippling now, colubrine, shedding flake after flake of old, dead life. Palm-sized red blisters slowly knit together into unblemished golden skin. Nearby, I hear five voices join together in choral song. By the time I have recovered enough to flip myself onto my side, they're in full, melodic flow. The sound is a current, pulling me toward them, but something dark and dirty seethes through the gaps in my mind. Pink welts mottle my arms, striping me tiger-bright. I crawl to kneel by the place where my lover died and dig my hands into the mottled patch of cordovan earth, my fingers spidering down as if there might be something to catch, to grasp, something that might be retrieved and relit. The blood smears the grass in a line east, leaving a path of crushed stalks for me to follow. *Growth happens in the dark too, Soph,* Eilidh used to say.

You lied, I think, my fists clenching, clawing great mounds of dirt into compact balls in my hands. *You lied.*

CHAPTER
SEVEN

I follow the bloody path through the grass and crawl towards the song. Stalks jab at my tender, new flesh, making me wince, though by the time I reach the Sunbathers, the pain has faded to no more than a mild sting. They're standing in open ground—and how strange that looks to me, since I've spent two years hiding and running and burrowing like terrified vermin—and their skin is luminous, their limbs well-muscled, their mouths each a deep red cavern from which the song, that endless, beautiful song, scours my soul and finds each and every impurity. I'm weeping, though it's not the awful, whimpering snot-fest I usually emit, but graceful, silent twin cascades wetting my cheeks.

When the song is over, they stare at me without speaking. Two women, both with the same kind of reddish hair as Cecily, their features too similar to be anything other than blood-related. Jacob stands on Cecily's right, while a short, white male Sunbather with perfectly white teeth and dark wavy hair grins at me. He could be anything from nineteen to thirty, and in the old world, that angular jaw and sharp cheekbones would likely have given him a fast track into modeling. They are so naked, so perfectly formed, so unashamed. Barefoot and barefaced, just as we once were thousands of years ago, just as we are again. *This is how things should be*, I think, a frisson of joy lighting up my chest like a single, shrieking firework.

The world is bleached of the most vibrant colours, leaving only a pale outline of the surroundings like a charcoal drawing, but that's no wonder, my eyelids were damn near singed off in the Burn. I blink, but nothing changes, nothing adjusts. It probably takes a while for everything to settle in. I clamber to my feet, feeling strength course through me. My hands curl into fists before splaying out again. My blood feels strange—white, and hot, as if I'm high. I can smell each of the Sunbathers as if each scent is a different texture; feathers, wood, velvet, polystyrene, cotton wool. The sound of voices turns my head. Someone is whispering nearby, their voice coloured crocodile-green. It takes me a moment to recognise Maya's voice, the sound so different to my new ears. Earthy, damp. Angry. Afraid.

The Sunbathers still stare at me, their chests rising and falling. I realise I have no idea what to say. What the hell does one say to a group of post-people who have long left their humanity behind? *What's up, fellow sun-lovers* doesn't quite seem to cut it, and an apology for being a worm up until about five minutes ago is only going to Other me more. I'm not even sure I can speak, anyway. My lips sting and my throat feels flayed. I feel the air of each breath whistling down through my sinuses into parched lungs, cracked like desert clay. None of them are holding so much as a cup of water.

"Welcome, sister," Cecily says.

"Welcome," the rest murmur, eyeing me with muted interest.

I croak something unintelligible in response. "Shh, don't talk," Jacob says. "It takes a while for the last of the weakness to drain away."

The tallest of the red-haired Sunbathers stares up at the sky. "When should we hunt the rest of the worms? Tomorrow?"

"They'll flee if you give them the chance," he reminds her. "Not that they'll get far in one night."

She shrugs. "I like the chase. It's been a while since we had a good—"

"I don't," Cecily says. "It's much more fun to dig them out. They squeal in a particular way that they just don't do anywhere else." A frown creases her beautiful face. "Despite my best efforts to recreate it."

She's talking as if the terror and pain are nothing more than a choice of appetisers, with much to recommend her own favourite.

"Either way suits me, sister. We can decide later." Jacob tilts his head, smiling. "Tomorrow, then."

The group turns and heads westward. They walk quickly, loping along with a peculiar gait that seems half-march, half-jog, and all grace. In contrast, I stumble along behind them on still-blistered feet. By the time I begin to smell the sea, that heady mix of sour-green-salt and keen-water-tang that can only be oceanic in origin, I'm able to move almost normally. The blisters on my hands and feet are entirely gone, though the ones on my upper arms and torso are still there. I reach up and rake fingers through my hair, feeling bumpy, raw skin splitting under the slightest pressure. It's not just my imagination— my dark, hickory curls are already thicker and more luscious. Though it's been months since I've seen my own reflection, I remember only too well the dark circles under my eyes, the wrinkles heralding my middle-thirties, the scars left from acne, all the places on my body which have willowed and wilted over time. I can't wait to see my glow-up, and the thought distracts me from the pangs of regret and shame over what I sacrificed to achieve such perfection.

I shake them off. Gods shouldn't feel guilt.

I've never been this close to a Sunbather base before, but I'm surprised to feel a thrill of dread coursing through me on approach; after all, I'm one of them now. As the group crest a sandy dune, I slow to a halt, staring open-mouthed at the scene below. A crowd of at least two hundred naked people, each a distinct, golden island, are joined only by a sea of sound and movement. They smell of textures —grainy, fluffy, glass-smooth—as if their scents are arriving in my brain via a non-olfactory part of me, creating a kind of grey absence where scent should be. It makes the hairs on the back of my neck prickle. They'd once smelled distinctly of lavender, but now my sense of smell, much like my vision, is bleached of what was once vivid.

I shake off my unease. I'm still recovering from the horrible ordeal of the Burn—I can't expect my body to adapt to a whole new way of life that quickly. The group descends the dunes, as sure-footed as goats, and I try to copy their movements, expecting to fall, though my balance is much better than I'd expected. When I'd thought of it at all, I'd pictured the Sunbather base to be ringed, fenced off in some way, but there's no physical boundary that I can see. Instead, small campfires ring a rough, shapeless area, set a little way back from the shore. A large bonfire in the approximate centre of the base blazes, producing a heat haze that makes the air around it shimmer. To the west, a treeless, rocky cliff rises steeply from the balding forest, overlooking the ocean at a dramatic height.

Tanning beds are clumped together in groups of seven or eight, encircling a large silver box. A cable runs from each, leading towards a large, stone-walled structure with no roof. I squint, wondering if that's where all the electricity is coming from. My understanding of basic engineering is no better than a child's, but even I know that they must need a decent amount of energy to power this stuff. In the near distance, another unroofed structure—though this one is much larger, the walls even higher—looms. I can't imagine what they'd use such a thing for, and my interest quickly dwindles.

At the furthest edge of the encampment, Sunbathers recline on lines of loungers only feet from the water's edge. Each of them holds something silver and reflective under their chins, their eyes closed in rapture. I notice that each lounger is just far enough for the occupant to stretch without touching a neighbor, and when my group moves through the crowd near the bonfire, they part for us. At first, I think it's because my captors are somehow important, but after a few moments of careful study, it's clear that the Sunbathers simply avoid touching each other entirely.

The baking air around the bonfire feels delightful, much like sitting in the highest part of a sauna. A soothing balm for my burnt, newborn skin. Despite my still cracked, dry throat, the hot air is somehow easier to breathe. Sunbathers don't have any need of tents or shelters, so everything is open-air, but there's a surprising lack of basic amenities. I know they sleep in the tanning beds, but where are their food stores? Where do they get water? I stare around, baffled, and almost bump into Jacob, catching myself just in time.

"Every day at noon, we conduct the Ritual," he says, a note of disapproval in his cold, unclouded voice. "Watch us closely, new sister, and do what we do. You will soon learn our ways."

I nod as we come to a standstill. The Sunbathers on the loungers get up and stand too. Murmurs among the crowd die down as the sun reaches its zenith. Silence, except for the wheeling screech of a gull in the distance. Every Sunbather stares up at the sun, so I do too. They stand frozen for long minutes, and just when I'm beginning to think that maybe there's nothing more to this ritual than staring, they raise both arms high above their heads like a salutation to their benefactor. The sun is my benefactor, too, I guess, since I survived the Burn. Glowing skin stretches over stacks of curved ribs, and as I mimic the movement I feel my own flesh stretching and absorbing the heat, the rays, the white-hot glory. I feel almost high on the energy, the light. Everyone moves in unison, their movements uniform, their arms lowering to their sides and up again.

I chance another sideways glance at the crowd. *Bloody hell*, I think, *it's WASP city*. There's not a single nonbinary or noticeably trans Sunbather in sight. Even if I assume that the Burn removes everything one no longer wants, and even if that included both primary and secondary sexual characteristics, I'd expect to see a little bit of androgyny in a group this size. At the very least, some obviously queer people. I'd pictured Zeus-esque muscled bears and smooth otters and diesel dykes with Hunger Games haircuts and fairy armadillos, but instead, everyone looks coiffed and cut and straight and goddamn preened to perfection, though I haven't yet noticed anyone doing any actual grooming in public. It might be a private affair, or perhaps personal aesthetics come naturally to a god.

Age, too, seems to span only three decades here. I see no one under the age of twenty, or over the age of forty in my immediate vicinity. Maybe the Burn eliminates the very old and the very young, or maybe they simply don't have the strength to endure such a thing.

The Ritual seems to take a long time to complete—an hour, maybe more—and by the end I'm impatient to move, to explore a bit more, though I have to admit that I do feel energized. The atmosphere lightens and people murmur to each other again, bestowing glowing smiles in every direction.

"Here," Cecily says, offering me a piece of foil.

Though it's not exactly a mirror, I can see a decent, if grainy reflection. A dark mane tumbles around my face, my jaw no longer a bow but a perfect curve. My eyes are a striking dark blue, glowing within the amber palette of my face. My nose has shrunk slightly. My lips have plumped up. It's like getting instant plastic surgery without the side effects. All-natural, homegrown beauty. *The sun giveth and it is a generous overlord indeed.* I grin at myself.

"Come," she adds, and I trot along obediently behind her. She gestures to a sun lounger and I sit, aiming the foil at my face to reflect the sunshine. It feels incredible, like the most delicious thing I've ever eaten in my life is being poured into every cell and absorbed. My jaw drops. I've heard heroin described like this, a glowing, rosy fog of bliss sliding through your veins, taking away every discomfort, but holy fuck, I wasn't expecting it to feel quite so incredible. I sigh and stretch, luxuriating in the feeling.

Cecily nods approvingly, and I'm disappointed that she leaves without another word, but extremely delighted to watch her walk away. "Welcome," a Sunbather on my left says. I turn to find the handsome boy, bronzed and beautiful, splayed on the sun lounger next to me. "You should rest as much as you can now," he continues. "You'll want to be at peak strength for the Flowering."

I raise an eyebrow. "Wait and see," he chuckles. His eyes are a vivid, cornflower-blue. His teeth are Lego-square, like neat suburban houses. "I'm Max."

My hand jerks out before I remember the rule, the human impulse to offer to shake hands still running strong. He laughs, his eyes traveling the length of my body. "Maybe later."

I smile politely and tilt my head back, closing my eyes. The heat is sweltering, but I delight in it and crave even more. I can feel the weight of Max's eyes on me, and an uncomfortable prickle runs the length of my spine. *Every soul stands alone,* Jacob had said. The Sunbathers don't touch anyone unless it's their Chosen One, whatever that means. *It's fine,* I think, pushing my unease away. *I can be monogamous. I've done it before.*

But you can't be straight, a little voice in my head reminds me.

Too fucking bad, I tell it. I'm in the light now, and nothing is going to pull me off the path. This is what I wanted, after all. This is what I murdered my girlfriend for. Take a dick now and again to live as a powerful, near-immortal god; it seems like a small price to pay, really. Besides, I'm sure there must be some queers around here who'd be willing to sneak off and screw in secret. They can't all be completely hetero. A tiny seed in my chest puts forth a single, aching shoot. Eilidh's eager mouth, her tender love, her fingers entwined with mine like she'd meant it. *No. Don't think about her,* I warn myself, and for the next few hours, I give myself over entirely to the radiant glow of my new life.

When the sun begins to descend, my body fluctuates too. I'm still powerful, still strong, but it feels like someone has turned an internal dial from ten down to a high six or low seven. The feeling is disconcerting, though my fear that it's only happening to me is quickly allayed; the Sunbathers around me have become quieter and more solemn. Not that they're ever exuberant. I can't remember ever seeing any of them whooping or screaming or expressing any kind of extreme emotion. It's all very straight, very beige, very aspirational-middle-class-Americana.

Apart from the cannibalism, of course. And the nudity.

One of Cecily's red-haired sister-cousins appears and leads me over to a tanning bed. The outside is a white, polished shell, hinged with brass. The bottom is lined with a soft white blanket. I climb in and feel instant relief at the bright, barred sunlight. "Wait," I say, and push back against the closing lid. "How does this work, exactly?"

"UV rays."

"Yeah, I know that but, like, how?" I persist. She shrugs. I wait, but she just stares at me blankly, then turns and wanders off. *Rude bitch.*

I lie back and let the lid close. It's my own fault for never paying attention to how basic things work. Before the world ended, I used to have a recurring nightmare about traveling back in time; when they discovered I was from the future, people would pester me for details of new technologies, and I'd be humiliated by being forced to admit that I didn't really know how something as easy as a toaster worked. The peasants or courtiers, depending on the particular era of the dream, would usher me into a forge or workshop, surrounded by metal parts, and I'd stand there, baffled, totally unable to reconstruct even the most basic modern appliance. The hot pyroclastic flow of panic would meet the cold front of disappointment, creating a maelstrom of humiliation. I usually woke up, sweating, horrified, and had to resist the urge to immediately look up and memorise the internal workings of a fridge.

I lie bathed in the brightness of the tanning bed and try not to picture Eilidh's face. I'm glad I didn't turn around, at the end. I'm glad they dragged her away before I saw what had been done. I have everything I wanted now, even if it cost me everything to get it. *What I gave up was nothing compared to what I gained,* I reason, *so it was all worth it, right?*

Absolutely. Definitely.

Right?

CHAPTER
EIGHT

In the morning, I'm woken by the low beep of a repetitive alarm, followed by the clanking and creaking of two hundred lids, all opening in unison. I open my own lid and stare blearily out at the base. I didn't sleep well, though I suppose it would be too much to hope that there's coffee; what need have gods for such human things?

I climb out of the tanning bed, shivering. The sun is only a couple of fingers high above the horizon, bright but not scorching. My movements are groggy and slow, and while the air is warm, it's not enough to energize me like the Ritual did yesterday. The Sunbathers are noticeably slower this morning too, their movements sluggish. Though animal biology was never a strong point of mine, reptiles come to mind. I can't remember the sciencey word for cold-blooded, but I do recall that their cold blood means that they require heat and light to energize them enough for basic functions like digestion and reproduction. *Jesus, so, what—I can't eat or fuck until the sun rises a bit more? Seems like a design flaw.*

I don't recognize anyone around me, so I sidle through the crowd, careful not to touch anyone, until I reach the other side of the base. Jacob and Max are sitting around a campfire while two other

Sunbathers are busy taking a body apart. Though they and the corpse are bloodied beyond recognition, I'd know those black braids anywhere. *Maya.* My flinch isn't for her, but for Eilidh, though another glance confirms that Maya is the only body present. I ignore the frisson of relief and watch, intrigued, as they unlimb her, skin her, and spit her meaty thighs over the fire. "Friend of yours, right?" Jacob asks, noticing my curiosity.

The two bloody Sunbathers get up and wander down to the sea. They don't splash themselves or even attempt to wash but simply wade to a place where the water is chest-height, then wade back to shore to drip dry. I raise an eyebrow. "I wouldn't call her that. Where are the others?"

"Kaia got her way, after all," Max adds, beaming widely at me. "She does love to hunt. What is your name, sister?"

"Soph," I say, dragging one of the nearby deckchairs over beside them.

"Sophie or Sophia?"

"Just Soph," I say, plopping down. I don't miss the flicker of disapproval on Jacob's face, but what-the-fuck-ever, that's my name. *Cope, dude.*

I make sure I'm close enough to the fire to feel the heat singeing my shins. Weirdly, I haven't been hungry or thirsty since I turned. I probe inwards, examining the interior of my body. Every sinew feels strong, every vein hearty and hale, every bone as solid as concrete. My vision is still weirdly bleached, making the orange flames of the campfire look more like a pale cantaloupe than a tangerine-bright shade. Jacob's skin looks almost grey rather than the crow-blue-black shine I remember seeing as a human. In contrast, Max's tan looks like an overly-milky latte. I remember my desire for coffee and supress a sigh.

We sit in silence for the next half an hour while the meat grills, the only sounds that of the crackling fire and the spitting, bubbling flesh. I'm positioned perfectly to view the buildings at the other end of the base; it might just be my imagination but the two Sunbathers loitering around outside the most distant building appear to be guarding something. Occasionally, someone ducks in or out of a wide door, carrying pieces of what looks like metal or tools. *Maybe the power source requires a lot of maintenance, or it's something to do with the tanning beds*, I figure. After all, if they fail to work for even one night, we're all toast, so I'm glad to see they have a system.

The sun rises steadily, hammering down on my exposed skin, and by the time the meat has turned an appetizing brown, I feel bright and alert. A pretty Sunbather—real blonde, with eyebrows so pale they fade into the overall shade of her face like a predatory fish hiding in the sand—offers me a section of Maya's thigh on a chipped floral plate, along with a handful of almonds and some figs. I don't want to be rude, so I accept the plate and they watch me while I take my first bite of flesh. Maya tastes different from the arm I found at the previous Sunbather's campsite, which feels like a million years ago now, though I don't know whether that's because Maya is different or I'm different, or both.

"How does it taste?" Max asks.

"Good." I chew, analyzing the texture and flavour. Juicy, sweet. It's not as meaty as the other one was, though she was a vegetarian so maybe diet has something to do with it. "So, how many do you need to catch to feed everybody?"

Jacob cocks his head, staring at me. "Need?"

I blink, mentally review my question and find nothing wrong with it. "How many worms do you usually catch when you hunt?" I rephrase, wondering what part of my previous sentence confused him.

He shrugs. "That depends. Sometimes a dozen, sometimes one."

I picture the Sunbathers—sturdy, athletic, indolent—working out the finer points of agriculture. "I didn't think you—I mean, we—were the farming type."

"We're not."

I decide to stop pussyfooting around. "Then what happens when there are no worms, or when you only catch a couple?"

"There are always worms," the blonde Sunbather says, waving a dismissive hand. "Here you go." She hands a section of Maya over to Jacob.

"Thank you, Victoria." Jacob's slight frown clears. "Did you think we need to eat wormflesh to survive?"

"Uh..." I lower my plate. "Don't you?"

They titter as if I've said something hilarious. "Of course not. We don't need to eat at all. We only need the sun for sustenance, and a very small amount of water."

"We only hunt worms for fun." The blonde Sunbather giggles again. Her accent is distinctly Scandinavian. "Imagine thinking that we need them for anything. We've evolved so far beyond that."

The squelchy, mushy lump of Maya's flesh slows to a halt on my tongue. The shock is cold and absolute and vertiginous. *What the fuck?* I've never been so wrong. I thought they were the ultimate in human evolution, the apex predator, the crown on the throne of the food chain. Now I see the truth—they're not better. They're only us, just more so.

"It is important to put them down, however," Jacob adds. "We don't want their numbers to grow enough so that they can fight back. Not that it would matter much, of course—we're vastly superior. But a single loss of our glorious company is a terrible waste."

Something's wrong, I think, forcing a smile, and choking the lump of meat down. *I shouldn't be feeling this way. I should be happy that I'm one of them. I should understand everything. I should be grateful.*

But I'm not.

As much as I desperately don't want to undergo another Burn, I'm worried that I might need to, since the first one clearly didn't sear away all my weaknesses. I don't want to bring it up yet, though. I'm still so new to all this. Maybe everyone feels this way to begin with and gets over it in time. *Maybe the second Burn won't be so bad,* I reason. I'm already much stronger than before, and if the first Burn didn't kill me, then there must be something worthy inside me, buried like a tick. I just need to dig down and connect with it, then kill whatever weakness is left with fire.

Cecily appears on my right before I can come to a decision either way. I can't help but admire her body—the rest are attractive, certainly, but there's something about Cecily's curves that really rev my engine. It almost reminds me of—

Fuck, don't think about Eilidh. The lump of meat I so recently swallowed threatens to make a reappearance. I focus on Cecily's tits, her toned stomach, her wide hips. She looks like a swimsuit model, seamless and showy, and though there's no actual scent to her, I get the impression of feathers, downy and soft.

"Sister!" Jacob greets her, with far more enthusiasm than I've seen him show before. "How was the hunt?"

Cecily jerks her chin and we all crane in that direction. A distant figure is dragging a long, lean body along the sands. *Cygnet.* "A good day's work, brother. We gave this one a chance to endure the Burn, to scorch away all their deviance, but they would not submit." She rolls her eyes. "Such perversions go soul-deep and are not easily removed."

Perversions? I think, puzzled. *Cygnet was actually pretty decent, considering our situation. Like, noble and selfless, but not a dick about it. Maybe it's just the worm shit again, like, non-believers are all going to hell, that kind of thing. Classic Othering.*

"Indeed," Max agrees, his boyish smile containing just a smidge too much canine for my liking.

"What was done in the dark cannot always be undone in the light," Jacob adds. "We shall glory in the Flowering in a few days to banish such impure degeneracy from our minds."

Max's eyes slide over my body. Between his muscled, golden thighs, there's a twitch of movement. "Do you have a Chosen One, Sophie?"

I clench my teeth but don't correct him. "She only turned yesterday," Cecily points out. "She doesn't even know what a Flowering is."

"We mate under the full heat of the sun," Jacob explains, in response to my baffled look. "It is a ritual and like all rituals, it requires cleanliness, sacrifice, and adherence to a strict code."

Well, that sounds like a super fun shag. "So what do I—"

"If you feel you are ready," he interrupts, "then you may join the procession today. Though there is no rush, and no one will think badly of you if you decide to wait until our next one." His voice drops to a purr. "They do happen once a week, after all."

This is beginning to sound like a scheduled chore rather than an orgy. "You don't do this Flowering thing here on the beach?"

"No," Cecily says. "We journey to the top of the hill. The movement itself is a holy one for us, for the sun set the hill ablaze long ago and nothing remains but the soil. It is an appropriately barren place in which to plant ourselves, and it is there that we give of ourselves to the sun." Her eyes glaze over for a moment, soft and unfocused, before they sharpen on me. "Do you feel ready for such a thing?"

I hesitate. Maybe a Flowering is just what I need, rather than undergoing a whole second Burn. If my soul is exposed to the sun—whatever the hell that means—then surely whatever weird human thing has been left inside me will shrivel up and die. This might be the last piece of the puzzle that I need in order to leave my old life fully behind and embrace my godhood. "Yes," I say, more confidently than I feel. "I'm ready."

CHAPTER
NINE

The hill is in fact more of a small mountain. As a human, I would have struggled to climb it without several breaks, but instead the Sunbathers jog up at a quick clip, moving in two well-spaced lines along the broad dirt path. I don't feel out of breath for even a single moment; if anything, my muscles are screaming for me to flex, to break into a sprint, to exercise some of my newfound energy. The sun is high in the sky, and since we've already performed the day's Ritual, there's nothing to do but jog and breathe and stare at the pert, bare asses of the Sunbathers directly in front of me. My soles slap the warm dirt with a steady *thwap-thwap*. Sunlight is all around, cocooning us in warmth, seeping into my pores, filling me with liquid ecstasy.

Godhood is the most dangerous drug, addictive and glorious.

"And how goes the lamp?" says the Sunbather beside me.

My ears prick. No one has yet mentioned the lamp to me directly, so I'd almost forgotten it existed. It's possible that they're nearing the end of the construction, or have already recruited enough people to work on it. I glance at her, curious. Though the question was aimed at

Victoria—the one who fed me a piece of Maya—she notices my interest and smiles. "Welcome, sister. You're new, aren't you?"

Black hair, greenish eyes, high cheekbones. She's gorgeous even for a Sunbather, and though I know I can't smell any of the Sunbathers, I can't help instinctively sniffing. The sense of red roof tiles, warmed by the sun, arrives in my brain. "Yes, I am. Thank you," I say. *Is it my imagination or did she just look at my tits?* "I've heard about this lamp, though I haven't seen it."

"Few have." She flashes a dazzling smile.

"It goes well, Thea," Victoria says, tucking a stray strand of blonde hair behind her ear. "Jacob thinks we should be finished in a month, perhaps two."

Thea raises her eyebrows. "Wonderful news."

"Forgive me for asking," I say, adopting their odd way of talking, though it makes me feel like I'm auditioning for a Blitz-era play. "But what exactly is it? I mean, how will it work?"

They exchange quick looks. "Well," Victoria speeds up slightly so that she's closer and can lower her voice a little, "The Lamp," she pronounces it with emphasis, as if it's capitalised, "will use concentrated UV rays to exude permanent, powerful illumination. No more scurrying and hiding away when darkness falls. Instead, the shadows will retreat before us. We'll be a conquering army and our weapons will be made of light."

"UV? Like the tanning beds we sleep in?" I frown. If that's the case, surely it was easy enough to build a really big version, though I can't picture how that would work. *Ah, that must be what that big second building is for*, I think, *though it seems a bit pointless to guard it. Who would be stupid enough to try to sabotage something that will make us even stronger?*

"Not exactly," Thea says. "There are different kinds of light. UV is only part of the spectrum, and while some of the existing light rays do nothing for us, UV is extremely beneficial in all its forms. You've felt the majesty of the sun, surely?" I nod. "Well, it can be split down into different kinds," she continues, "which are more or less effective, depending on the type."

Ahead of us, a brown, flat summit rises above the treeline. The sky beyond is a glacial blue, pale as molten silver. The murmur of the Sunbathers, reverential and hushed, sounds like a great wind gliding through a forest.

"UV used to be about ten percent of the entire solar output before the solar flares became common," Victoria adds. "Now it's much more. Picture it, sisters. There will never be darkness again."

"Won't that be wonderful?" Thea smiles, though for a moment I think I see something in her eyes that isn't entirely happiness.

I smile in agreement, though I'm filled with sudden trepidation. If this lamp comes to fruition—and why wouldn't it—then I'll never see true darkness again. Never stare up at the stars, the vastness of space. Never close my eyes and see anything other than the red glare of a summer afternoon, never see the silver glow of moonlight touching everything with fairytale wonder. I shake off the strange feeling, unable to put a name to it. *Nostalgia? Remorse? Whatever. What difference does it make?* We're already masters of the day, though the lack of darkness is already beginning to gnaw on my nerves a little. *I'll get used to it, just like I'm getting used to everything else.*

The summit is a wide plateau, as barren as Cecily said it would be. The Sunbathers who have already arrived stand in single male-female pairings. I expected this to be an exciting moment, crackling with anticipation, but it's surprisingly bland for a pre-orgy gathering. Max strolls over and presents himself in front of me, beaming like he's picked the choicest cut of meat at the butcher's shop. I smile back; so much for being able to choose a partner. His cock, wide and slightly flattened, is already rising to bridge the gap between us. I have an irresistible urge to grab it and shake it like it's a hand—as if he's interviewing me for an admin job in some corporate hellhole—and have to bite down hard on my lip to turn my laugh into a mere smirk.

He smiles back, holding me at pink gunpoint.

On some unseen and unheard signal, the women lie down on their backs in the dirt. I mimic them, the warm soil dry and pleasant against my skin, and before I can ask any questions about what I'm supposed to be doing, Max is on top of me and inside me. No foreplay, no kissing, just a steady thrusting rhythm in and out. A quick glance informs me that everyone else has adopted the same missionary position to the same steady beat. Behind Max, a brown-haired man in his mid-thirties—more pretty than handsome, with an obvious hole in his left earlobe where a piercing used to be—has his eyes screwed shut as he humps his willing blonde partner.

I wince, feeling dry skin rub against dry skin, and picture the changes I'd make: foreplay to get us hot, in honor of the sun. Oral required from the men for at least several minutes. Moving the pairs into big circles, so that every woman could be tonguing the ass of another while she gets fucked, like a sexy human centipede. This list helps finally spark a flicker of interest, and while Max pumps away, admiring the muscles of his own toned stomach as they shift and surge, I slide my hand down to touch myself.

He moves my hand away.

I move it back.

He moves it away again.

I stare into his dazzling blue eyes, rage building in my stomach. *Are you for fucking real?* He stares resolutely at his dick, his brow furrowed in concentration. On my left, Cecily is getting fucked by Jacob, and on my right, Thea, whose eyes unexpectedly meet mine. She looks away first, staring up at the sky, but I can see her eyes flickering back in my direction, sliding over my body as her bland-faced partner screws up his face in soulful focus. *Interesting.*

It's over in minutes, and the air is full of the groans of male Sunbathers, finishing like exhausted marathon runners, clambering to their feet with all the victorious arrogance of Olympians.

"You're welcome," Max says, grinning like he genuinely thinks he's given me the best sex of my life. "Can't wait to do this again next week."

I stare up, baffled, as he wanders off. I used to think I hated myself—and I suppose I did—and that becoming a Sunbather would cure me of that self-loathing, but so far, all it's made me feel is even more hollow than I did before.

"Sister," Cecily calls, watching me climb to my feet. "Now that the Flowering has sated us, we have an appetite for the hunt. Care to join us today?"

Sated us? I think, trying not to pull a face. *I've never been further from coming in my whole life. Can't I even have a wank in peace?* I stare around, but everyone looks pleased with their performance. Thea, a bright smile plastered to her face, is studiously avoiding my eye. "Of course, sister. I would be honored to hunt with you." After all, I've nothing better to do than sit around, let sun-heroin seep into my skin, and eat bits of my former acquaintances. It's not exactly the hedonistic, dynamic Paradise I'd imagined, and every day that I exist as a Sunbather is simply another day that strips away all my former notions about how amazing life as a god might be.

On the way down, I stall long enough to join the back of the line beside Thea, who looks less than happy about jogging next to me. "Did you have fun?" I ask, and her quick jaw clench is enough to confirm my suspicions. She doesn't answer, her gaze darting from side to side, though the Sunbathers in front of us are too engaged in their own conversation to pay attention. I lower my voice. "Why don't we slow down and get to know each other a little?"

"We don't perform deviant behaviour here, sister." Her body is tense, coiled.

I start to say *you're kidding me, right?* but I see the look on her face and I stop. She's serious as a heart attack. "Of course. You misunderstand me—I have no impure intentions."

Like hell I don't. Sweat prickles down my spine. The muscle jumps in her jaw again. She's silent until we round the next bend, and then she whispers, "They'd kill us for even talking about it. They'd pull the power to our beds and leave us to die out here in the dark. And it's not a quick death." She shudders. "I've seen it happen."

I bite my bottom lip, feeling frustration boil low in my belly. "Not worth the risk. Got it."

She opens her mouth to add something else, but the Sunbather in front turns. "Thea, do you think salt water helps us burn more? I swear when I've splashed some sea water on, I can feel the difference."

"Actually yes," she says, sounding relieved at the distraction. "And there are flowers, too, like St John's Wort, that can actually—"

I tune out of the debate, staring at the tides of golden, naked bodies in front of me, descending in two currents. *Fuck,* I think. I've given up so much and gained so little.

What use is being all-powerful if you can't do whatever you want?

CHAPTER
TEN

I join up with Cecily's crew at the bottom of the hill. Her redhaired sister-cousins—I don't care enough to find out their names or remember them—nod to me. They've been joined by two men, neither of whom I remember seeing before. One peers out from under a shaggy, seventies, Bee-Gee-esque mane, while the other has the kind of neatly combed white-boy-hair most often seen in films from the fifties. I spare a single wistful thought for the death of movies—an art form which had existed for more than a century and a half, and had disappeared in mere months after the first Burn—and trot along beside them. To my recollection, nobody has ever spoken of the before-times—not our families, not our jobs, not our hobbies. It seems somehow uncouth to bring it up, but it means that I struggle to get a grip on what their personalities might have been, and what they definitely aren't now.

"Isn't it a little late in the day to be hunting?" I ask, casting a suspicious glance towards the sun. If I had to guess, I'd say it's about three or four in the afternoon, and though the light will be good for hours yet, I'm all too aware of our noticeable decline in power before sunset.

"We already know where we're going," Cecily explains. "There's a big group, at least seven or eight of them. Migrating westwards. Dale's been tracking them for weeks." She nods towards the Gibb-brother, who puffs up with pride. "We assume they're heading for the harbor."

I blink. That had been Eilidh's idea too—evade the Sunbathers, steal a ferry or something equally absurd, sail off into the sunset for a happily ever after; how easy she'd made it sound. "There's a harbour?" I keep my tone light, curious, slightly stupid. Better to give them the impression that I'm slow and shallow and incapable of original thought.

Or sin.

"Oh yes." One of the sister-cousins nods. "Every so often, a group makes a break for it. We always catch them, of course,"

Cecily turns and jogs a couple of steps before breaking into a full sprint. The rest dash after her and I panic, wondering how the hell I'm going to keep up but before I can protest my body settles into a perfect pace, legs pumping, arms pistoning, and I'm flying over the ground with ease. The scenery blurs past smears of bleached earth-tones, my feet bounding with caprine confidence with every step, my muscles screaming with relief that all that pent-up energy can finally release, even if its not the kind of release I'd prefer, and—

Christ. This is almost as good as the sunlight drug. In some ways, it's even better. I never want it to end.

By my calculation, we cover six miles in about nine or ten minutes, and come to a halt about two miles south of where my old territory ended; a while back, I'd recognised two gnarled trees, leaning as close as old lovers, which had marked that boundary. This is the first exertion since I turned which has left me feeling even slightly winded, slightly alive. Though I know we're here to hunt, part of me wishes that we could simply run forever.

Cecily holds up her hand. We halt in our tracks. The others raise their noses, scenting the still air. I do the same, though I'm not sure what they're looking for. Soon enough, I catch it. Human: warm and meaty with a hint of smoke. It's a relief to actually smell something, and I sniff again, trying to drink it in, savouring the aroma. The others have wrinkled their noses in distaste and I copy the expression, keen to be seen as normal. Cecily moves forward noiselessly, the muscles of her back flexing with coiled tension.

We hear the worms long before we see them. Either their whispers carry further than they realise, or my hearing has increased triple-fold, or both. I expect to see them but all that's visible is a hole in the ground, about five feet in diameter. At first, I'm not sure what's going on, or why they're so close to the surface at this hour, but then it hits me. They must have stopped before dawn and dug this hole themselves rather than pushing on to the coast in broad daylight and attracting attention. A sensible decision, in ordinary circumstances, but today is not their lucky day.

Cecily beckons the Sunbather with the neat hair forward and signals to the rest of us to wait. Immediately, the rest fan out, covering all positions, waiting to catch the prey once flushed. *Tale as old as time*, I think, and slide into the largest gap, half-crouched and ready. Mr Neat Hair pounces first, dragging two humans out, one in each hand. They're both young, in their early twenties at most, and their feet drag through the dirt before he holds them up by the hair. The girls squeal in panic while Cecily beams as if it's her birthday, and I'm reminded of what she said days ago about preferring to dig out trapped worms rather than chasing them. A man lunges out of the hole and tries to grab one of the girls' dangling, kicking feet, but Cecily hauls him up and snaps his neck, dropping him bonelessly into the dirt. Mr Neat Hair adjusts his grip, a hand around each neck, and begins to squeeze. While the girls' faces purple, their scrabbling hands clawing at every part of him they can reach, Cecily turns her attention back to the hole. "Come out, come out, whoever you are," she sings, and her voice—as exquisite as diamond and just as cold, just as shiny and untouchable—prickles the hairs on the back of my neck.

It's a bloody, brutal affair. The hole is just shallow enough to let her sister-cousins catch the next three without much trouble, and just deep enough so that the remaining couple of worms linger at the back, inches out of reach and protected by the dark. While the Bee Gee and the sister-cousins giggle and taunt a crying worm, his broken legs dragging uselessly behind him as he crawls away, Cecily circles the hole, tapping her bare feet against the withered grass, listening for something. "Here," she says, and stamps hard. The ground gives way under her foot, caving in. Kneeling, she reaches down, then retracts her hand, hissing. Dull teeth marks are imprinted on her golden skin. I expected to see blood, but instead of the expected stream of red, something white oozes from the bite.

I don't really think about what I'm doing, or whether there's any kind of safety protocol, group hierarchy, or any rules to this chaos. I just lunge forward, grab whatever I can hold, and tug. The darkness stripes my forearms with pain, and though I expected it—knowing what our weakness is—I didn't expect it to hurt so much. The first blush is beautiful, like the sting of a leather belt, but the feeling blossoms into a wider, redder agony. I yelp but hang on grimly. The man who comes sliding out is sixty if he's a day, grey at the temples, sinewy and strong. He's wielding an axe, which surprises me so much that I'm too startled to realise I should let go. I'm saved from losing a hand by Cecily, whose fist hits the side of the man's head at a speed even I can barely make out. One moment, his expression is furious and terrified and vengeful, and the next he has no face at all, just a gaping red hole ringed with bubbly pink flesh.

I drop his leg and it hits the ground with a heavy thud. Now that I'm not facing imminent dismemberment—and for all my powers of strength and regeneration, I don't think total limb regrowth is included in the deluxe package—I'm free to notice details. His body is dressed in lightweight fabric of the kind of green-grey colour that blends easily in forest landscapes. I'm shocked that guys this old have lived this long, but then I see the scars on his neck and arms and I understand. *If he lived long enough to scar, he lived long enough to learn.*

I'm impressed. It's almost a shame they have to die. If not for Dale's keen interest, then this group might well have made it to the harbour and whatever safety lay beyond the sea. To my left, the worm with the broken legs cries out, his wails escalating into high-pitched screams. Cecily is smiling down at me, her chin smeared in blood from where she's absently scratched it. "Well done, sister," she purrs. "And what about the last one?" I nod but there's an odd bubbling noise from the darkness, followed by the distinct iron-rust, sharp-bright smell of blood. "Boo," she pouts. "It's no fun when they don't play the game."

"What do you think, Dale?" One of the sister-cousins bats her eyelashes at him. "Should we bring this worm back for roasting?"

Dale's smile is that of a benevolent patriarch. "Whatever pleases you, sweet one."

The worm whimpers. *Christ, he's not dead yet. Why don't they put him out of his misery?* I get my answer quicker than I'd like; Dale picks up one broken leg and sprints off, the worm's blurry body dragging behind him. The rest of the Sunbathers follow one by one. I do the same, having no wish to hang around here and bask in the aftermath. I thought it would be more noble, somehow. Triumphing over the worms, our superior strength and skill giving us the clever advantage. The reality is gory and grim and a bit grimy if I'm honest. Like shooting chickens in a coop. What sort of glory is that? *Maybe I would have felt better if I'd actually got to kill one.*

On the way back, I fall further and further behind, though none of them seem to notice or care. Veering east, I speed up, hurdling walls and fences and low bushes with leonine grace. I can't go back to the camp right now; I have to take a minute and put my thoughts in order. Something drifts in the wind. The scent of panic, as sharp and silver as a mirror. I skid to a halt as they come over the nearest rise. Two of them—a man and a woman. The man is wearing the same green-grey fabric as the worms we killed earlier, and he's about the same age. The woman is much younger, though not much faster, darting through the sparse trees, trying to stick to the shade. A rabbit, staying one leap ahead of a fox.

Here's my chance.

He's too focused on her to notice until I'm practically next to him, and his reactions are too slow to matter. I kill him by kicking his legs from under him, toppling him onto his back, and then punching through his skull so hard it cracks like an Easter egg around my hand. I pick off the shards of bone before wiping the blood and goo off on the grass. Now I'm really one of them. Now I'm really a killer. Yet where I'd expected to feel triumph or happiness, nothing is swelling inside me.

"Go on, then," the worm says, her hands on her knees, her breath coming in sharp, raw bursts. Her accent is exactly the kind I like—southern, lilting, a little too yeehaw to be really pretty. My toes curl into the dry grass. "Finish it. I'm so fucking tired of living like this."

I hesitate. Euthanasia hasn't exactly been part of the Sunbathers training manual. Besides, I'm not going to do anything a sodding worm tells me to do. If she wants to die, then I'm going to force her to live as punishment. *Perfectly sound logic,* I reason. Definitely nothing to do with her hair, which is tied back with a rainbow band, or her cuffed jeans, or her sweat-stained t-shirt which I recognise as a queer band I used to love.

"Who was he?" I jerk my chin towards the body of the guy. "Your boyfriend?"

"No." She shrugs, and I see truth written in the lines of her body. Disgust curls her lip as she glances at the remains of the man. "He found me yesterday. Started following me. Wanted more than I had to give."

She stares at me, her eyes defiant and brimming with tears. Realisation dawns. "Oh," I say. At least the Sunbathers, fucked as they are, don't do that. They'll gut you like a deer, sure, and suck the damn marrow from your bones for funsies, but they don't seem to have any interest in doing anything outside an extreme narrow margin of predetermined heterosexuality. Only animals mount without consent, without concern. A spark flares inside my chest, a flame guttering uncertainly. Maybe I did make the right decision after all. I stare down at his body and give it another kick. "Sorry, or whatever."

"Like you give a fuck. You're a long way from home, English."

Is she trying to goad me with some casual xenophobia? "Why don't you join us?"

She laughs, incredulous, and straightens up. "Are you trying to recruit me?"

Something about her reminds me of me, reminds me of Eilidh, of something she could never dig deep enough to find and something I could never seed long enough to bloom. I stride forward and slap the woman, hard. She gasps, but the sound isn't all pain. I cock my head. "Did you like that, worm?"

"Maybe I did." She swallows. Her pupils have dilated, her tongue darting out to wet her lips. "What's the matter, killer? Don't they fuck you often enough over at Cannibal Barbie Beach Camp?"

There's enough truth in her words to sting. I slap her again, harder. "You're nothing but filth. You don't deserve to live."

"That's weird because you just saved my life," she points out. My handprint has risen on her face, red-fingered and sharp, and the sight flips something inside me. The air between us crackles. I lunge forward and kiss her hard, and she makes a startled sound, her teeth grazing my lips. Hands snaking around my biceps, squeezing the hard muscle there, the still-tender burns the darkness of the worm-hole inflicted on me. The hiss catches in my throat and curdles into a moan of pleasure.

Her accent comes out more pronounced, her voice rough with arousal. "I thought y'all didn't—"

"Shut up," I order and, surprisingly, she does.

After a quick glance to ascertain there's no one around, I drag the worm into the nearest piece of part-shade, revelling in the pain. The worm whimpers, her skin covered in a pretty chessboard of light.

Patchwork person, like a doll. She could be my little pet. For the first time since I turned, I feel the unmistakable ache of lust, tar-black and sticky-sweet. *Christ, I want to come all over her.*

I lose myself in the relief of her mouth, wet and eager, her slender fingers, the shape of her body curving just so under me. She's barely touched me and already I'm dripping, arousal dribbling down my thighs. The shadows burn me but the sunlight through the shifting leaves soothes the sting, and she's moaning under me, her face buried in my shoulder, her teeth sinking into the golden flesh there and everything Max didn't give me comes roaring up in a tumultuous blaze and—

Afterwards, I lie there, feeling the aftershocks like ripples in a pebble-struck pond, each a distinct circle, fading into nothing. I turn to say something, though I've no idea what, but my attention is caught by a flower, sheltered in the base of a large tree, trembling in the slight breeze. I blink, baffled to find I can see how vivid it is, how purple. The colour takes my breath away. *What the fuck*, I think, and roll to my feet in one graceful movement. Did screwing the worm do something to me? Contaminate me? My immediate reaction is panic, rage, and fear, but the flower is beautiful, so vibrant, and Eilidh's favourite colour was purple and *don't think about her don't think about her don't think about what you did don't think—*

I roll into the sunlight and sigh with relief. The worm is propped on her elbow, her chest rising and falling, her cheeks flushed with exertion, her eyes tinged with fear. I could kill her to keep my secret, though it's not as if she's going to tell anyone. Besides, if I kill her, then I can't fuck her again, and without an outlet for my desires, I'm going to lose my mind. I rise to my feet, stretch, and eye the sun. I better be heading back. They'll wonder where I've been, and I'd rather not be interrogated too closely, not after tainting myself.

"Try not to get yourself killed overnight. I'll see you here tomorrow." My voice is steady, though something inside me is whirling, lost. "Same place. Same time."

Her eyebrows disappear into her hairline. "And what if I don't come?"

"You're all alone and there's nowhere for you to go. Don't kid yourself, worm." I chuckle, my eyes raking her body. She shivers under that look. "You'll come."

CHAPTER
ELEVEN

Over the next couple of weeks, whenever I feel like I can risk it, I sneak away from the Sunbathers base and screw the worm. Each time I do, more colour is restored to my vision, painting the bleached-charcoal-drawing landscape with increasingly vivid technicolour. I can't complain—I missed seeing reality in real shades, missed the withered chartreuse grass, missed the bright yellow of flower pollen peeking coyly from skirted petals.

The human stink of the worm's armpits, musky and sour, has evolved from a craving to an urge to an addiction. During the unavoidable once-a-week Flowerings with Max, I keep myself entertained by imagining the worm's open mouth, the pineapple-sweet stink of her human skin, her stupid, imperfect body with all its regular sags and wrinkles and moles and bruises and, Christ, it's so raw and real that it makes me lose my mind. Max stands over me, beaming, every time he finishes. He's evidently proud of what he probably sees as his own improvement over the last month, though he hasn't actually made me come yet. Sometimes I picture him catching me sinning, the worm fucking me better than he ever could, the hurt on his face slicing bone-deep. The thought pleases me in a way that no part of Sunbather life has ever managed to do.

It's not all fun and games, though. With improved vision comes clarity of a different kind. Feelings I'd hoped to never experience again arrive first as slow waves breaking against the shore of my consciousness, and soon swell into horrible floods of overwhelming negativity. At night I weep in my tanning bed, the tears drying on my cheeks in salty tracks. I dream of Eilidh's final cries ringing in my ears, of all the terrible and callous ways I treated people around me, of the casual cruelty with which I lived my life. In the morning, I'm forced to plaster a happy, sunny smile across my face and saunter about the base as if there's nothing wrong, as if I'm not crumbling on the inside. I could stop screwing the worm but I can't bring myself to cut it off. The more I fuck her, the more I understand that feeling awful is an apt punishment, and not nearly a tenth of what I deserve.

Besides, she has great tits.

Today I bring the worm a hunk of meat, grilled to perfection. "Thanks," she says. She didn't thank me the first couple of times, evidently wondering whether I was planning to poison her, but now she's too hungry to care. Or maybe she actually trusts me, which would be stupid. I watch her eat, watch the grease drip down her chin, feeling my pussy twitch with anticipation. "Who was this?" she asks. I shrug, a twinge of blue remorse stirring in my withered heart. She sighs. "Better that I don't know, I suppose."

The last bite disappears into her mouth. Before she's finished chewing, I flip her onto her back and leave a trail of wet kiss-bites along her thighs. I've undergone the Flowering several times now and still, I can't give up the desire to fuck women. *What is so deep-rooted in my soul that it can't be burned out?* I wonder, my tongue swiping down in a broad, slow stripe that has the worm arching her back with a deep groan. There may in fact be no real line which divides the bad me and the good me. *Maybe I'm just unfixable.* It shouldn't be the worst idea in the world, but something about it has burrowed down into my bones and nested there, eating me from the inside.

While I'm wrist-deep in the worm, trying not to think about spitted meat or who it might have previously belonged to or which exact part of me might be broken beyond repair, something flickers in the trees. The non-scent of roof tiles, smoothed by the seasons, wafts on the breeze. *Oh shit, that's Thea.* I pause my ministrations and turn my head, scanning the trees. There—on the right, just where the sparse grove ends. Dark hair, touched by sunlight. Green eyes, wide with shock. I tense, waiting for her to dash off to snitch on me, but instead, she inches forward, holding my gaze. Her hands drift, one south to six o'clock, one west to ten o'clock. She rubs her nipple, tweaking and tugging, her head tilted to one side as if trying to figure out the answer to a complicated question.

I turn back to my task, which doesn't take long. The worm shudders through her orgasm and doesn't waste a single moment before she grabs my face and hauls me up, kissing me hard, pressing her tepid body against me. Cool fingers, slender and sure, press against me, into me, dipping and teasing and stroking until I clench my eyes shut with a final gasp.

When I open them again, Thea has already disappeared.

Back at the base that afternoon, Thea corners me as I stand on the beach, watching the sky turn a brilliant, bloody orange. "You didn't see me today," she says, low and urgent. "And I didn't see you, okay?"

"Sure."

"This isn't… I mean…" Her swallow is audible.

"My lips are sealed." I can feel the weight of her stare on the back of my head. I bend over, pick up a shell and pretend to admire it in the light. "That being said, maybe next time you could join us instead of wanking fervently in the undergrowth. Just a suggestion."

There's a brief silence. "How the hell did you ever make it through a Burn?"

I repress a snort, though she has a point. "The sun's choices are not ours to question, sister." I throw her a lascivious look over my shoulder as I strut away, leaving her slack-jawed and swallowing hard.

During the next Flowering, I lie next to Thea, close enough to feel her breath on my face before she turns and stares up at the sky. Close enough to hear her stuttering breath as the male Sunbather on top of her thrusts with dogged determination. Close enough to see her close her eyes when he finishes with a shrill howl and to know exactly what she's picturing instead.

OF COURSE, Thea is there the next time I visit the worm. I feel her presence before I see her, smell the same non-scent I've grown used to. I don't actually expect my fellow Sunbather to do anything, not after what she said the other day, but she surprises me by stepping forward and clearing her throat. The worm stills under me, a noise of alarm sounding low in her chest, but I pet her hair with my free hand and she mewls with delight. The sound visibly electrifies Thea.

"Where do you want me?" she asks, her voice low and uncertain.

This is the first time I have ever actually felt like a god. I lift the worm, who weighs little more than a couple of bags of flour in my arms, and lay her so that her head and shoulders are in the sun. "Kneel," I say, guiding Thea over the worm's face. She does, and the worm doesn't need any instructions, but goes to town immediately, eagerly licking and sucking every inch of flesh within reach.

I reach under Thea's chin and gently tug her face towards mine. Her mouth is open, and though there's a moment of resistance, she gives in to the kiss so quickly that I wouldn't have noticed if I hadn't been looking for it. Her moans are soft but real, and I realise that through multiple Flowerings I've never heard her make a single noise before. She makes up for it now, thrusting against the worm's face with ragged, desperate thrusts. "God, yes," she breathes, green eyes ablaze with desire, and the worm hums enthusiastic agreement.

I grab the worm's left hand, since her right is busy hanging on to Thea's thigh, and press it between my legs. "Good girl," I breathe, as two then three fingers sink inside me.

The next few minutes are spent in perfect, triangular harmony. Thea's hands clutch at my shoulders, cup my tits, slide up into my hair and pull hard enough to hurt. I grin, wondering how long she's wanted to do that, how long I've been living in her head rent-free, and order her to do it again. She obeys without question, and I bend forwards, angling so that I have access to her neck. I nibble my way up and down, my hands sliding over the worm's stomach, her soft flesh so different from ours. My knee is pressed against the worm's legs and from the twitchy jerk of her hips as she grinds against me, I can tell she's already close.

I'm having so much fun, I don't want it to end. I consider edging the worm for a while, but Thea's chin drops to her chest, her hand curving around my bicep for support, and she comes with a cry that startles several birds from the nearby trees. I console myself with the thought that there will be other days, other sessions, and let my own climax build to its usual frenetic conclusion.

Thea collapses onto the grass and stares up at the trees like she's never seen them before. "What the hell?" she breathes. Her pupils are blown, obscuring the vivid green of her irises. I catch the slightest whiff of something under all the fear. Floral sweetness, like dying roses; maybe that's her true scent. "I can see the leaves. They're so... why are they so—"

Ah, so the colour thing isn't just me. I wave a dismissive hand while the worm rocks herself to a quiet, shuddering climax against my leg. "Don't worry. That happens."

"Does it fade?" she asks.

"I think it's more like something growing back. The dark doesn't hurt me quite as much either." I've been experimenting at night by carefully sticking one finger, then a whole hand, outside the safe zone of my tanning bed, though to what end I don't really know. Boredom exasperates the mind and makes it do weird stuff. "It still hurts like a motherfucker, don't get me wrong. It's just not quite as bad. Could be handy, someday. You never know when—"

"Can they smell the change on us? Can they tell?" Her face, normally a beautiful tan, has paled with terror.

"Well I've been screwing her," I gesture to the worm, who's eyeing Thea with renewed caution, "for weeks now and no Sunbather has said shit to me, so no, I guess not. They're not exactly 'live and let live' types, are they?"

My words do nothing to calm Thea down. She clambers to her feet, her hands shaking. "I have to go. I have to—"

She takes off, sprinting. I let her leave. *Walk it off, girl,* I think, rolling my eyes. *It's not a big deal unless they find out.*

The worm cocks her head. "You never talk about the changes. I didn't know—"

"It's not any of your business." I sprawl out in the sun, letting the light fill my every pore. That sickly-sweet feeling, the drugged-up haze, seems so artificial next to a good old-fashioned burst of orgasmic dopamine. "Besides, there's nothing to tell. Colour vision came back, I feel stuff again sometimes. So what? No big deal."

"I can see it written all over your face," she says. "You hate being one of them, don't you? Don't think I don't know that they haze people when they have the time and inclination to play with their food first. What terrible thing did you have to do to become one of them?"

Maybe it's the change. Maybe it's my own stupidity. Either way, when I should be telling her to shut the fuck up and stuffing her mouth with something useful, instead I bite my lip. "I'm a Sunbather. All my sins have already been burned away."

"You don't believe that shit any more than I do. Any fool can see it's rotting y'all from the inside," she says, as casually as if we're talking about what to order for lunch.

"That's—" I hesitate. "That can't be true, because there's nothing inside me." A lie, but not a distant one. A cousin to the truth, really.

"I see you," the worm adds. "I see your shame." I roll my eyes.

This is the most we've ever spoken, and it was clearly a mistake to let her start mouthing off. "Who was she?" the worm persists.

From the tone, I know she's not talking about Thea. "Fuck you."

Her eyes narrow, nostrils flare. She's got the scent now. *Shit.* She crawls over and tries to kiss me tenderly, but it's not genuine. Behind the sweetness there's a rank bitterness that stings, humiliating me. I twist my head away and get up and brush blades of grass off my shins to hide my discomfort. I really don't want to talk about this.

"Come on," she says, getting up. She faces me, her body dappled in shadow. "Be real with me for once."

The silence drags on, but she refuses to fill it. *Fine. What's the old saying—be careful what you wish for.* "I... I killed her," I admit. "The woman I loved. Okay? Are you happy?"

"What do you mean?" She doesn't look quite so sure of herself now.

"They told me I had to kill what I loved in order to be free. So I led them to her and I let them murder her. That was the price I paid to join the Sunbathers." Bile rises in my throat, but the words keep coming. "Lamb to the slaughter and all that. Really fucking biblical."

"Christ on a stick," she breathes.

"So it had better be worth it, right? Because otherwise my girlfriend—my loving, sweet, innocent girlfriend—died for nothing, right?" I'm on my knees now, screaming in her face, but she doesn't back away. "Tell me, worm! How could that be possible? Explain that paradox to me!"

To her credit, she hardly flinches. "The paradox of... what, exactly? Being a cunt?"

I slap her so hard she flies back, sprawls on her ass in the dirt. She turns her head and hawks blood into the soil. It lies there, less a puddle than a tiny bubble of scarlet saliva. "If I'm so fucking *good*," I spit the word," then how could I have done something so fucking awful?"

"You're crying," she says, in a tone that sounds almost like wonder and reaches for my face.

I want to launch her right into space, to lift her high and break her spine over my knee, to punch through her chest and rip out her heart and carry it with me all the way to the sea where I can drag it down into the deepest fathoms. Instead, I let her touch me, and the tears come thick and fast and my hands are covered in the blood blooming from her split lip and I understand that my heart has always been a splintered, shattered thing and that I've always been a barreling trainwreck, broken beyond repair, and that not even the sun, the almighty sun, has the power to glue me back together.

Quite a thing, to be unfixable even by a star. Yet it doesn't make me feel unique, or special.

It makes me wish I was dead.

CHAPTER
TWELVE

Back at the base, Thea is nowhere to be seen. I expected to see her making eyes at her Chosen One, throwing herself guiltily back into the hetero trappings of our wonderful little cult, but her guy is sitting alone on a sun lounger, tanning himself into further oblivion. At least, I think it's him.

I shrug, and wander over to where Max and Jacob are sitting. *Once Thea gets used to the colour bleeding back into her life*, I reason, *she'll come around*. What's her option otherwise—settling for getting railed once a week by a guy so boring I can barely even pick him out of a crowd?

That night, I get into my tanning bed and find that my demons are a little quieter than usual. Maybe it's a result of the fun threesome, or a sense of new beginnings, or finally confessing what I did to Eilidh, but either way, I drift off into a contented, deep sleep, and awake in the morning feeling more refreshed than I have in weeks. When the alarm goes off, I'm slow to rise. I take a moment to picture yesterday, a slow grin spreading across my face at the memory of moans and tits and beautiful shades of green, before the sound of voices draws my attention. The tone is all wrong—panicked, confused, angry—and I instinctively push up the lid, roll out of the bed, and hit the floor, assuming we're under attack.

We're not. A group has gathered at the ocean's edge, staring at something on the sand. For a moment I think it must be a beached baby whale or a dolphin or something that survived the repeated boiling of the oceans, but as I trot closer I see dark hair. A limp, tanned hand. A body, bloated, but not yet beyond recognition.

"Brothers and sisters," Jacob is saying, his hands held up to quell the noise. "Who among us has some knowledge of investigative work?"

I frown, not sure what he means by that, but Victoria steps forward. "I was a coroner in the before-times, brother."

The Sunbathers exchange looks. I try to picture Victoria in scrubs or medical whites and come up blank. "Good," Jacob nods. "What can you tell us?"

She kneels and moves Thea's body this way and that. "No obvious signs of an attack. No cuts, scratches, or bruising."

"Poison?" Max suggests, leaning forward with interest.

"Unlikely." Victoria probes Thea's mouth. "No discolouration of the tongue or skin. Besides, how would you convince one of us to eat or drink when we don't need to?"

"The worms might have poisoned themselves before we caught them," someone calls. "A trojan horse."

The crowd murmur. Cecily holds up a hand and they subside again. "We will stop consuming worm flesh for the time being. In the meantime, let us be on our guard for any other signs of enemy activity."

Jacob smiles at her. "Perhaps we should consider ridding the area of worms entirely. Just to be on the safe side. A pestilence can so easily grow into a plague."

"A wonderful idea," she agrees, and my heart hammers so hard I'm surprised they don't hear it. In just a few short minutes I've gone from having daydreams about threesomes to having even my own worm rooted out and killed. Without her, I'll stop changing. I'll be stuck, like this, forever. She's the only thing that's tethering me to reality as it actually is, rather than this shallow, perfect, Barbie version. And yet, if I choose to protect the worm, then I'm picking a side—a side I already actively renounced—and going up against the entirety of the Sunbathers. *So much for new beginnings.*

"Do not forget that we are almost finished with the Lamp," Jacob announces, and relief shows on the face of every Sunbather. "With our great project completed, the filthy worms will not be able to use darkness to their advantage and we, dear friends, will never have to worry about our one weakness ever again."

I move amongst the crowd, nodding and offering words of consolation like the rest, and when I'm sure no one is looking, I slip out of the base and run like the wind.

THE WORM, when I tell her everything that's happened, frowns. "What do you mean, a lamp?"

"I don't know. That's just what I heard. And it's not just a lamp, its *the* Lamp. Like, the Lamp to end all lamps. No more darkness, ever."

She opens her mouth to snark, and then thinks better of it; a new, not unwelcome development. "Shit," she says, after a few minutes of silence.

"Yeah."

"That's... not good."

"Yeah," I agree.

"Why are you telling me?"

I blink. "Why am I telling you a secret, or why am I telling you, specifically?"

She hesitates. "Both."

I pretend to think about this, although I already know both answers; they're not comfortable ones. "Because I think it signals the absolute end of humanity, and there's... there's something in me that doesn't want the human race to end, even if I chose to leave it behind to become something new." I shift and roll my shoulders, but the discomfort remains. "And because I have nobody else. Because I let them all die. Because being a Sunbather means being alone in a crowd. Everything we do is for the greater good, for the overall group, but it's a…" I wave my hands. "Like… a whitewashed way to live. Blank. Smooth-faced. Bloody *tabula rasa*'d. Whatever! It's fucked, is what I'm saying."

"Okay." She bites her lip. "So, what do you know?"

I stare at the purple flower at the base of the tree, which has been joined by two tiny green shoots. So delicate, so fragile. Yet life finds a way to survive, even in the most perilous times. "Just that they're building a Lamp. That's pretty much it. They have a building near the base, but no one is allowed to go in without specific permission."

"You weren't curious? Y'all never tried to sneak a peek?"

"No. It didn't really matter to me before."

She gives me a long, calculating look. "And it does now?"

"I… I guess so." I huff. I'm definitely not picturing Thea, alone on a cliff, shivering in the face of truth. *We could have had fun. We could have been happy. It's not my fault.* I remember the last time I told myself this very same lie and my stomach curdles. "What do you know about electrical engineering?"

She shrugs. "Very goddamn little. But I do know that blowing something up usually renders it good and dead."

I pull a face. "Sabotage would be more subtle."

"Sabotage can be fixed. Explosions can't."

She has a point, though I don't have to like it. "I wouldn't even know where to begin. Like, how do you blow something up?" I complain. "Light a fire? Three?"

"We're in agricultural country here, you know."

"So?"

She rolls her eyes. "The tractors and shit probably still have fuel in them. Bags of fertilizer are flammable. We'll make do with whatever we can find."

I cock my head. "We?"

"You'll need help," she says. "Besides, you're a stone-cold bitch, but I think there's a heart in there somewhere. And I appreciate that you don't want to end humanity as a whole, even if you're not one of us anymore."

"Great speech. Really encouraging."

"You're welcome, killer." The look in her eyes is surprisingly soft. "If you want a way to redeem yourself, this is definitely it."

"I never said I—"

"You didn't have to." She leans over and kisses me, soft and slow, and for once I don't resist.

THE FIRST FARM I stop at has floral curtains and several deep, dark smears on the slabs outside the front door which look like they've been baked right into the stone. A couple of tractors have been abandoned in the fields, the furrows long picked over by animals and birds. The vehicles themselves have been corroded by the sun, their paintwork bleached so much I can't tell what the original colour might have been. I yank off the cap and bend over it, sniffing. It stinks of old metal and hot air, and only the faintest whiff of fuel. I curse and throw the cap into the driver's seat. Another tractor, partially shaded by the house, yields better results. I rummage through the tools in the nearby shed, find a length of tubing, and perform the gravity-suck-trick the worm promised me would work and which I'd only ever seen happen on shitty cop shows and once in a low-budget porn. I manage to get almost half a can filled before the trick stops working.

The second farm is a total waste of time. At the third farm I find four boxes of long stemmed matches and manage to get another almost full can of fuel from some kind of harvester thing. At the fourth farm, I find bags of fertilizer piled high inside an intact barn. I heft as many as I can carry and bring them back to the worm. "You'll have to carry them much closer," she points out, struggling to lift two at once. "There's no way I could shift all this by myself."

"I don't want to risk them finding anything. They'll assume it's humans and go on a rampage."

"No different than usual." She shrugs. "It's a risk we'll have to take. When do you want to do this?"

"Tomorrow, I guess." I help her drag the bags into her burrow. "The later I leave it, the more danger all the humans will be in. The more danger you'll be in. Can you swim?"

"Since before I could walk."

"If shit goes south, go around the cliff. The tide won't be in for a while yet and it'll make your journey to the harbour that much faster. If you can make it there, you've got a good chance of getting out. Can you drive a boat?"

"Rich people do it, so it can't be that hard." She grins. "I'll figure it out. What about you?"

"What about me?"

Realisation dawns on the worm's face like a sunrise, slow and inexorable. "You want to be bait?"

"It makes the most sense. They won't expect it and they'll be too mad to think straight." I raise an eyebrow. "Pun intended."

"This is serious," she chides. "What you're suggesting is suicide."

"I know." I pull her close, something I've never done before. She wraps her arms around my waist and rests her cheek on my shoulder. "I can hold them off long enough for you to set up your pyrotechnics. But you'll have to be quick and you'll have to get out of there even quicker. Once it's lit, run and don't look back."

"Okay, okay, I hear you." She sighs. "Damn, I was just starting to like you, too."

"No, you weren't," I murmur, and though the snort of laughter gusting over my skin isn't enough to make me shiver, a cold prickle travels down my spine anyway.

CHAPTER
THIRTEEN

I return to the base just before noon, but Cecily appears before I can join the crowd, who are already staring up into the sky in anticipation. "Where have you been?" she asks. "You almost missed the Ritual."

I stare up at the sky, doing my best to exude placid serenity. *Nothing to see here.* "I wanted to get a start on tracking this morning, to see if I could pick up any trails or anything. I couldn't just sit around and do nothing. Not after..." I trail off and let her fill in the blank.

In my peripheral vision, her shoulders relax. "It's terrible what happened to Thea, isn't it? Just when you think you've seen the worst of what the worms are capable of." She shakes her head and, imbuing my expression with the genuine sorrow I feel about Thea's death, I meet her gaze.

"They're monsters." My tone comes out quivering, but luckily she seems to interpret this as a rush of sorrow rather than fear.

"Oh, sister. I understand your pain." She purses her lips. "Don't you worry. We'll make them pay tenfold what they took from us."

Ever since I started fucking the worm, the Rituals have been torture; not quite as bad as a Burn, but definitely agony, and I have to spend the entire hour pretending I'm having the time of my life while my eyes sting from the glare. The rest of the day is a thousand years long, and by the time the sun begins to dip, I've talked myself in and out of the plan hundreds of times. Ultimately, my always-healthy sense of self-preservation is overruled each time by the simple fact that had Eilidh been in my position now, she would undoubtedly be cooking up something equally noble, equally selfless.

Equally stupid.

I'm pulled out of my reverie by a commotion on the edge of camp. Three Sunbathers are dragging in a fourth, who's kicking and bucking the whole way. *What fresh hell is this?* I wonder and gather with the rest.

"We found Diego liaising with a worm," one of the captors calls, pushing dark hair out of his eyes. They throw Diego on the ground and he lands as gracefully as a cat, springing to his feet. If I had to guess, I'd say he was in his mid thirties. Brown-haired, black eyebrows, with a pointy elven face and a formerly pierced earlobe. I recognise him from my first Flowering; he was the only man within my field of vision with his eyes closed. I wonder exactly what he was picturing instead of missionary with his female partner.

Cecily steps forward. "Liaising, Thomas?"

The dark-haired Sunbather nods. "I wouldn't sully your ears with details, sister."

Convenient, I think. It could be anything from necrophilia to queerness to a consensual hand holding and I'm guessing the punishment would be the same either way. Leniency is not part of our code: kill or be killed, eat or be eaten, burn or be burned. Jacob appears, the crowd parting to let him through. No one has ever actually referred to him as our leader, but it's clear that he has claimed the unspoken title anyway. With his bulging muscles, handsome face, and impressive stature, he's the natural role model for Baby's First Patriarchy. "What do you have to say for yourself, Diego?"

"It was a mistake," Diego blurts. "I'm sorry, Jacob." He stares around at the crowd. "I'm sorry. I'll be better, I swear. I was just hunting, and I got so lost in the bloodlust and then I... it was an accident. I didn't mean—"

"What happened, brother," Jacob asks, "when you endured the Burn?"

Diego swallows, hangs his head. "The sun scorched the sins out of me."

"And this is how you repay that kindness?"

He's openly weeping. "I'm so sorry," he burbles. "Let me Burn again, brother. Let me prove my loyalty. I swear—"

"No, no," Jacob shakes his head. "I think it's too late for that." Diego's face pales, his eyes wide with panic. "Liaising with worms?" Jacob clucks in faux consternation. "You know what happens to traitors around here."

"I'm sorry," he screams, dropping into a cringing half-crouch. "Please!"

"Unfortunately, I don't believe you," Jacob says. The crowd is silent; I can't hear so much as a breath. "Let's see if the sun does." He lifts a cable attached to a nearby tanning bed and flexes, snapping it in half. Electricity crackles as he lets the cables drop onto the sand. Diego howls in panic and terror. "And if one bottle should happen to fall," Jacob half-sings, smirking, then glances up at the sky. "At least you won't have long to wait. Goodnight, everyone."

The people around me move towards the tanning beds and begin climbing inside. Puzzled, I follow them and get into my own, though I keep the lid cracked so I can see what's happening. I don't quite understand why they don't just kill Diego now, or why we're going to bed so early. Diego rushes from tanning bed to tanning bed, trying to find an empty one, trying to pull people out of theirs. From behind, Cecily—armed with a long blade—stabs him in the guts twice before neatly stepping out of reach. The dimming light has weakened us all, though her knife goes in easily enough. He screams, clutching at his back. White blood trickles freely from the wounds just above his kidneys.

The realisation hits me like a freight train. They're going to leave him to die alone. This isn't a murder; it's a slow execution.

The rest of the Sunbathers close their lids as Diego runs, panicked, from one to the next. I close my own lid and fasten the inside clasp, which I've never had to do before. Diego's frenzied howls make me feel sick. The sound of his desperate fingers scrabbling and clawing at the closed lids remind me of an animal caught in a cage. What a strange subversion, to be encased in a safety cage, while the outside world fills up with darkness and death.

I flinch as Diego scratches the side of my bed, trying to haul the lid open. I follow the noise left, then right, as he proceeds to try every single lid at least twice, like a sick version of Goldilocks where nothing suits at all. The sun must have almost set by now. I'm sweating, bile rising in my throat. If I throw up in here, too bad. I'm not opening my lid for anyone.

Thudding on the sand. Heavy footfalls. A body slumping over.

Is that it? I wonder, relief billowing in my chest. *Is it over?*

And then the screams begin in earnest.

IN THE MORNING, Diego's body lies between two tanning beds, his arms reaching out for both of them. His skin shines like a film negative, his hair now chalk-white. Dribbles of white blood from his nose, mouth, ears and eyes have congealed. His jaw is open, but slanted sideways, as if he died mid-scream.

It's awful. It's horrific. I can't stop staring at him. None of us can.

"Let this be a lesson to all of us," Jacob declares, as two Sunbathers drag Diego's body over the unroofed building. One of them fetches a hammer. "Those who walk in the sun must be careful never to step into shadow."

I nod along with the rest, but my stomach churns. I swallow down the bitter, yellow taste of remorse. Now I see why Thea jumped—better to drown than to burn alive. Better to die quickly by your own hand instead of this lingering torture. Better to blow this whole fucking world up rather than endure it a single second longer. The plan the worm and I made is the right decision; I see that now. All I need is a decent distraction and I can slip away quietly.

"I don't think any of us should leave camp today," Cecily suggests, while the Sunbathers nail Diego's limp corpse to the wall. "We could all benefit from a nice long Ritual to affirm our faith in the wake of this disloyalty."

"What a wonderful idea," Jacob agrees, and everyone around me murmurs assent.

Well, fuck.

CHAPTER
FOURTEEN

Pre-dawn on the following day, I slip out of my tanning bed and bite back a hiss as the dim light stings my skin with a thousand little needles. Experimenting with an arm was one thing, especially when I knew I could retreat into the tanning bed, but the whole-body experience feels like I'm on bloody fire. Too bad —if I don't go during this brief window, I risk screwing up the entire plan. I creep out of the base, then sprint to the worm's hideout. She's already waiting for me, and looks both furious and relieved to see me. "What the hell?" she snaps. "You were supposed to be here yesterday."

I spend a couple of minutes explaining what happened the day before. "It was a total shitshow and I couldn't leave without raising suspicion. We need them caught unawares."

"Jesus. Apology accepted."

I ignore both this jab and the fleeting insinuation that she might have been worried about my well-being. "So there'll be a guy nailed to a building, okay? But that's not where they keep the Lamp. You want to go to the other one."

"The building without a guy nailed to it," she says, deadpan. "Great. Anything else I should look out for?"

I shrug. "Don't ask me. You're the explosives expert."

The next twenty minutes are spent on two trips—one to carry the bags of fertilizer and hide them behind the building which houses the Lamp, and one to carry the cans of fuel while she clings to my back. The rising sun is so low that it's agony to run at full pace and much harder to carry the bags which had felt so weightless in the full light of day. I keep to a decent pace, though it's nowhere near my fastest speed since I don't want to tire myself out before the real race begins. I halt just before the low rise of the dunes and let the worm off my back.

"Right," she says, after dropping down, staggering dizzily, and retching a couple of times. "Let's do this."

"Wait," I say, grabbing and holding her wrist before she can move out of reach. "I never asked—what's your name?"

She smiles, her voice deepening into that sexy rasp I've grown fond of. "You don't really want to know that, do you?"

"No," I admit. "I guess I don't."

"Well done." She leans over and presses a kiss to my mouth, cool and tender. "That'll be the last honest thing you'll have ever said." I grimace, and she laughs. "Good luck, killer," she adds, and hares off over the field. I watch her disappear into a small copse of trees only a few hundred metres from the Sunbather base. I sigh heavily. *This better fucking work.*

I take my place on the top of the low rise and wait for the daily alarm. The beeping begins sooner than I'd like and is followed by the sound of two hundred lids creaking open. Blonde Victoria is the first to spot me already out, already standing. Her jaw drops and, one by one, every Sunbather head turns in my direction.

"I killed Thea," I announce. It's not a lie, not really; I'm indirectly responsible. "And I'd do it again, too." I clear my throat. They're all staring at me, mouths hanging open in shock. "So, yeah. Fuck you, and fuck your stupid, boring sun shit. Come and get me, bitches."

It's hardly Churchill, but it'll do. I'm just wondering whether I should repeat it or insult them when Thea's Chosen One screams and hurtles towards me. A second later, the others pour out of their beds and swarm up the low rise. I turn and run like hell, the landscape blurring around me. As I leap a fence, I chance a look back. The entire Sunbather army are right behind me, and they're not nearly as sluggish as I'd banked on. I barely stay abreast for the first few miles and only manage to put a little distance between us once I've pushed myself to my limit. My muscles scream like never before as I lead them across the country with no real idea where I'm going. In my head, I count the seconds; I just need to give the worm long enough to get in and do whatever she needs to do. After another four miles, I turn and streak back in the direction of the base. Someone snarls behind me—the pack, catching up, almost within grasping distance—and for the first time I misjudge my footing, stumble, stagger onwards at full speed. *Shit, shit.* Pain shoots up my left leg but there's no possibility of slowing down now. I lean into the agony, letting it take over my instincts, putting on a burst of speed as I pelt over the sand. Rays of scorching heat stroke my body, the sun gaining power as it rises. Grasping fingers brush my streaming hair.

The building is five hundred metres away.

Four hundred.

Two hundred.

Christ, I hope I've timed this right.

I bolt through the base just as the first explosion hits. The first wave of Sunbathers are caught in the next explosion and as I leap free, shrapnel slices my cheek and arms, spattering me with blood. I taste salt as I sprint, my chest burning, unable to help another glance backwards. The second explosion sends another group of Sunbathers hurtling in all directions. Screams fill the air. Limbs soar in every direction, propelled by blood. It's all happening so fast and I can't stop, have to keep going to—

The third explosion is the biggest yet, sending a mushroom cloud of smoke into the air. Billowing fire follows. One by one, the tanning beds begin to explode. I duck as pieces of metal hit the sand around me. I'm almost free when a shard hits me right between the shoulder blades. Cursing, I twist around and try to pull it free, but I can't get a proper grip with my bloody, sweaty palms. The remaining Sunbathers emerge from the cloud of smoke and fire; they look charred and oozy by turns, but that hasn't stopped them roaring with fury and fear. Jacob leads what remains of the pack, advancing across the beach with dogged determination. The sun is already rising, the sky a beautiful pink streaked with red. I stare out at the ocean, towards the cliff, and I'm sure I can see a tiny, dark shape moving at the base. *The worm made it*, I think, and the relief makes my legs feel shaky.

I slow down, letting the Sunbathers catch up to me. They slow, warily, the pack encircling me. Rage shimmers on their skin, making them glow even more golden and beautiful between their terrible wounds. White blood drips from each of us, drawing ragged circles on the sand. It's thrilling to see them brought so low, to see gods tremble before me.

"She destroyed the Lamp!" some cry.

"She destroyed the beds!" others cry.

They know now the terrible anticipation of death, for without the tanning beds to protect us we are mere mayflies, with only a single day left to live. I can see it in their eyes, the dreadful understanding of mortality.

No more beginnings. Only endings.

"Why would you do this to your own kind?" Jacob snarls, his pale blue eyes fixed on me. "Why, when the sun has given you much, would you betray it so?"

There's no answer I could possibly give that would satisfy them, but I tell the truth anyway. "I don't know, man." A giggle bubbles out of me, and it's hard to get the rest of the words out. "I guess this whole thing just isn't very... me."

Teeth bared, they attack as one. I can't stop laughing the whole time, even while I'm spitting white teeth and white bones and white blood, because in a way its so fucking funny and terrible that by choosing to actually give up my godhood—the godhood I gave everything up to achieve in the first place—I've done something meaningful for the first and last time in my life.

Eilidh, I think. Her face flashes before me with every blow: laughing, crying, kissing, dreaming, bathed in moonlight. *Maybe you can forgive me someday.*

When darkness finally falls, it's a blessing, not a curse.

Acknowledgments

Firstly, I owe the existence of this book to the wonderful Caitlin Marceau—I owe you endless gratitude—who read my original 'Sunbathers' story (published by *Cosmic Horror Monthly* in early 2024) and wanted more of that world. I'd also like to thank the team at *Cosmic Horror Monthly*, particularly editor TJ Price, who picked that story out of the slush pile and coddled it to their weird little hearts. My Hedone editor, Nelka Mazur, who worked with me to make Sunbathers 'the little train wreck that could', must be credited with both fantastic edits and some of the funniest comments I've ever read on a manuscript.

Thank you to my darling fiancée Z. K. Abraham, whose dreamy, beautiful work is a constant source of inspiration, and who patiently listened to me describing each new horrible twist and turn of the plot, even that one time I put us both off our lunch. And to my friends, who read Sunbathers and pretty much universally said "we love it but what's WRONG with you?" —I appreciate you all too. (And the answer, I think, will continue to be revealed piece-by-piece in book form forever)

About the Author

Lindz McLeod is a queer Scottish writer who dabbles in the surreal. Her short prose has been published by Apex, Catapult, Pseudopod, and many more. Her longer work includes the short story collection TURDUCKEN (Spaceboy, 2023), as well as her books BEAST (Hear Us Scream, 2023), SUNBATHERS (Hedone Books, 2024), THE UNLIKELY PURSUIT OF MARY BENNET (Harlequin/Atom, 2025), WE, THE DROWNING (Android Press, 2026), and the collaborative anthology AN HONOUR AND A PRIVILEGE (Stanchion, 2025). Her work has been taught in schools, universities, and turned into avant-garde opera. She is a full member of the SFWA, the club president of the Edinburgh Writers' Club, and is currently studying for a PhD in Creative Writing. Lindz lives in Edinburgh with her fiancée and two extremely photogenic cats.

DETAILED CONTENT WARNINGS

Sex scenes (including a graphic orgy)
Death
Murder
Cannibalism
Internalised and external homophobia

Made in the USA
Coppell, TX
25 October 2024

38811448R00063